KALEIDOSCOPE

An advance review of *Kaleidoscope*:

"After reading Kevin Berry's *Stim*, I couldn't wait for the second book in his insightful and entertaining Aspie series, and his second title *Kaleidoscope* doesn't disappoint. Set in the chaos and uncertainty of post-quake Christchurch, *Kaleidoscope* is a secret look into the diary of Robert's girlfriend and flatmate, 20-year old psychology student Chloe Wilson. Chloe is so likeable: zany—crazy even—with her splash of blue hair, talent for music and a penchant for witty neologisms. But having Asperger's Syndrome and also Bipolar Disorder, means Chloe craves order. She struggles to make everyday decisions which normal-spectrum people take for granted. If only she had a script for life which would eliminate uncertainty. So, when she's forced to cope with a new house, no transport, a lack of power and water, along with the disappearance of her kitten, and the fact that her cousin is listed as missing, and all without her meds, Chloe's life is thrown into disarray, with results that are both disastrous and droll. A remarkable story told with sensitivity, *Kaleidoscope* describes the despair that follows a tragedy. But, ultimately, Berry's message is one of hope, since out of chaos, anything is possible." – **Lee Murray, author of *A Dash of Reality*, the award-winning *Battle of the Birds*, and *Misplaced*.**

This is a work of fiction. Names, characters, places and incidents are products of the author's imagination or are used fictitiously and are not to be construed as real. Any resemblance to actual events, locales, businesses, organisations, or persons (living or dead) is entirely coincidental. The exception to all this is that the February 2011 earthquake in Christchurch, New Zealand, did actually happen.

Copyright ©2014 by Kevin Berry
www.kevinberrybooks.com
Twitter: @kevinberryxxx

ISBN-13: 978-1494780968
ISBN-10: 1494780968
Waspie Publishing

Cover design by Rebecca Berto, Berto Designs, bertodesigns.com

All rights reserved. No part of this may be used or reproduced in any manner whatsoever without written permission, except for brief quotations used in reviews.

This book uses UK spelling and punctuation conventions.

KALEIDOSCOPE

The sequel to STIM

An Aspie New Adult novel
set in an earthquake zone

Kevin Berry

ALSO BY THIS AUTHOR

Stim
The book preceding Kaleidoscope
Published October 2013

CHAPTER **O**NE

I've been stable on my current cocktail of medications for a while. Seven and a half months—the longest it's ever been. But it never lasts. I don't know if it's because these psychotropic meds are inherently unstable when mixed together (and supplemented with wine, green tea and Marmite sandwiches), or if it is because my body eventually works out a way to fight back against them. What I do know is that sooner or later something unexpected will happen, they'll stop working, and I'll go crazy again.

No, wait. Crazy isn't the right word. Crazy is the word I hear the whitecoats whispering when they think I'm asleep, but I'm pretending. But it's only me, the real me, the one they want to sedate. To tranquillise me. To calm me down. For my own protection, of course.

And the meds work, to a degree. I'm functioning. I'm not wild and unfettered, feisty and uncontrollable, freakish and unpredictable on the meds. And I don't get so down, so negative, that I just want to die. But neither do I have the extraordinary energy and focus and flashes of creative genius that are so pervasively intoxicating when they occur. Instead of my moods fluctuating from high to low erratically like the signals of a heart monitor linked to some Frankensteinian creation being brought to life, they are averaged out, almost flattened as if the heart monitor barely registers a pulse. That's me on the meds. More dead than alive, I think, sometimes. But not the real me, anyway.

My boyfriend, Robert, told me I should write a diary to record how I feel from day to day, though how I can describe it in words, I don't know. He also thinks I should write my life history, but I'm not going to do that. I have to live in the present, facing life one day at a time, so I'll write it like that. I don't know how I'm going to feel tomorrow, or even this afternoon, and I sure as hell don't remember how I felt last week or last month.

It feels weird starting this journal. Even more so because Robert stopped writing his own diary last year, not long after we started sleeping together. We'd been sharing a house as flatmates for most of the year with my cousin, Stef, and I always thought Robert was cute, but he didn't notice me, and he wanted a girlfriend who was 'normal', or at least typical. Not like me, for I'm certainly not. If there is a 'normal', then I'm the polar opposite of it.

I was too afraid to sleep by myself after the earthquake, in case it happened again. I just couldn't face being in the dark by myself, even though we made my bedroom safer so the bookcase probably wouldn't fall over again. So I slept in Robert's bed, with him. And I realised that I really liked him, and we had sex. A lot. I love him, truly, or at least I think I do, though I'm not entirely sure, because I don't know what love is, and anyway, how I feel about him changes from day to day. I don't know if he loves me or not, because he's never said so, or if he has, I don't remember it. And I don't ask, because he'll tell me the truth, and I'm not ready to hear that, whatever it is.

I don't know if anyone will ever read this diary (I'm going to keep it so well-hidden, not even Robert will find it), or if it will be coherent or lexically consistent or whatever an inquisitive reader expects it to be, but it's going to be my story, from now on. And I'll tell it in my own way as I see it through my weird perception, because I can't tell it in any other way. I experience the world through a filter like a kaleidoscope; everything's there, but all jumbled up. Jargogled like pieces of crazy paving in my mind's eye.

So this is the utterly unrestrained diary of Chloe Wilson, aged 20, about to start my third year at university. I'd include a picture, but I hate having my picture taken, so I'll describe myself. I like body piercings, so I have a surfeit of those—multiple earrings and studs, lower lip, right eyebrow and you won't want to know where else. I like a striking hairstyle, so I used to have my hair completely dyed blue. While away, I changed it so I now have just a large patch of blue at the front of my naturally black hair, covering part of the left side of my face, and matching blue eyebrows. The contrast in my hair colour makes it appear more dramatic. My eyes are a wistful blue-grey colour. People either stare at me, or won't look at me, and I don't care either way.

Why am I taking the meds? You may be wondering. Sometimes, I don't even know this myself. Like my boyfriend Robert, I'm an Aspie, which means I have Asperger's Syndrome, but that's not an illness, it's a neurological condition resulting in a pervasive developmental difference, so it's part of me. But that isn't why I have the meds. I have them because I'm bipolar. Without the meds, my moods fluctuate wildly and, sometimes, uncontrollably. That is what the whitecoats claim anyway, and my dad. He pays for my psychotherapy. But, over the years, the whitecoats have labelled me with diagnosis after diagnosis, each more exotic than those preceding it, including ODD (Oppositional Defiant Disorder), ADD (Attention Deficit Disorder), which I think is just ridiculous because I can concentrate on most things for as much as several minutes at a time, GAD (Generalised Anxiety Disorder), dyscalculia and various others that I don't even remember or never properly understood. I suppose it *was just a matter of time before they called me bipolar and drugged the wilder side of me out of me.*

I want to rediscover that part of myself. It is the real me, after all. I'm tempted to flush my meds down the loo, but I know that's not safe. It's actually friggin' dangerous to discontinue these meds abruptly. So, I'll wait for the right time to reclaim myself from the clutches of my pharmaceuticals and break free. I'll wait for a sign.

The guy in the seat next to mine freaked me out. It's a four-hour flight from Melbourne to Christchurch, but he didn't appear to have a kindle or other e-reader, or reading material of any kind. I hoped he planned to sleep through the entire journey, but no, he turned to me and grinned as if he'd recognised me as an old friend from somewhere. Maybe he intended to talk throughout the journey. I feel anxious about flying as it is without having to deal with this kind of useless social interaction. I need my book as an escape, as a little bubble of life-support, as a controlled environment around me to distract me from the fact that I'm surrounded by hundreds of strangers in a tin can in the air that I can't get off if I have a panic attack.

Red-faced and perspiring from the scorching heat of the late summer afternoon, I sat down and tried to stuff my oversized carry-on bag into a space too small for it under the seat in front of me. After only a few seconds, the suave, casually dressed guy leaned over, still smiling broadly. He talked to me. I didn't know why.

"Sure is a hot day out there," he said. I felt his gaze boring into me.

I didn't stare back at him. He had stated the obvious. Did he think I was so stupid that I did not realise how hot the day was, or was his comment some kind of criticism of my sweaty appearance? Was he actually saying that he has noticed I reek of sweat and city grime? What a *passenjerk*. Did his nose twitch just now? I tried to read his expression, but I couldn't. I almost never can read expressions accurately anyway, and especially not with my peripheral vision.

I decided that 'Sure is a hot day out there', which is a pointless statement by itself, must be a euphemism for something, or some kind of trite verbal fluff masquerading as an invitation to talk. Non-Spectrum people are always coming out with those, and I don't like them because they don't make it clear what the person wants. I prevaricated, unsure of how to respond. He seemed to be expecting a reply because he continued to smile in my direction. If he'd been complaining about me, he probably would've turned away by now.

"Angelo," he said, sticking his hand out. I glanced at it, but I didn't want to touch it in case it was unclean. Instead, I sat down and continued my battle with the bag.

"Do you live in Christchurch?" he asked. "Or are you going there for a holiday?"

"I live there," I said. I didn't see any reason not to tell him that, though I couldn't see any reason why he would need to know, either.

Finally, I finished wrestling with my carry-on bag and conceded defeat. There was no way using conventional physics that I could force the bag under the seat in front. Some of it poked out. I put my feet on it to try to conceal it so the stewardess wouldn't tell me to stow it in the overhead locker, out of sight. If it was out of sight, I'd worry about it.

Mere seconds later, my nose was assailed by a strong whiff of perfume and body odour, a vile mixture that smelled of chemicals, grubby sweat and what you get if you open the refrigerator after being away for a month and discover old opened yoghurt inside. I turned and looked up sharply. A meaty, large-breasted woman crowded into my space, hovering over me like some kind of ominous alien mothership. She leaned over, shook her boarding pass in my face, stared at me with beady eyes above a crooked nose and scowling mouth, and growled.

"That's my seat you're in. Thirteen-D."

"But it's my seat," I groaned. Her sickly fragrance made my head spin.

"Is there a problem here?" A stewardess appeared at the large woman's side as if by magic. "Oh, by the way, you'll have to put that in the overhead locker." She gestured at the carry-on bag under my feet.

I swooned, suffocated by the large woman's overbearing scent and by the way she leaned over me. I closed my eyes, leaned back in my seat, fished down the front of my top and pulled the boarding pass out of my bra.

"Are you all right?" said Angelo, paying me rather close attention. I ignored him.

"See?" I opened my eyes and showed the pass to the three of them in turn. My nausea worsened. The large woman stank worse than a colony of gannets sitting amongst the remains of their old fish dinners. I wanted her to go away.

"That says thirty-one-D," said Angelo.

"I told you this was my seat!" crooned the fat lady.

"You'll be towards the rear of the aircraft," the stewardess told me. "Here, let me help you." She pulled my tote bag from under the seat with one hand while offering me the other. I lurched to my feet. She took my arm and helped me along the aisle. At least the smell of the pregnant lady diminished with every step. I screwed up the boarding pass and stuffed it back into my bra. It's not a lot of use when you have numerical dyslexia.

Fortunately, I had a row of seats to myself near the back of the aircraft and would be able to stretch out comfortably. That somewhat lessened my *tripidation*. That's a neologism, meaning anxiety about travel. I smiled; I love using new words that I've found on the web or in the urban dictionary, or obsolete words that hardly anyone knows. That's one of my *idiosyncrazies*.

My cousin Stef met me at the airport after the flight landed that afternoon and I'd collected my checked-in baggage. I had bribed her with the promise of chocolate, so I knew she would turn up. We didn't hug, of course. Stef knows I am often uncomfortable with physical contact in public. We said 'hello', and Stef asked me about my flight, which allowed me to expunge the horror of it by dumping it on her. She paid a lot of attention to my changed hairstyle and said it suited me.

We walked through the airport, following various detour signs that led us through temporary walkways constructed to allow people to navigate the airport refurbishment work safely. I looked around at the unfamiliar surroundings and tried to imagine what it might be like when it was finished. I didn't like change, but it is much easier to get used to when it is drawn out slowly like some kind of organised chaos, instead of happening all at once, unpredictable and confronting.

Construction work blocked off the main entrance, and we followed a tunnel of plywood to a side door that opened to the car park. From there, we had a short walk to The

Frog. That's Stef's car, a little green thing with a faulty clutch that hops and jerks along the road. The only reliable thing about it is its unreliability, but Stef somehow manages to get it moving in some manner most of the time.

I threw my bags into the boot, then we got into the car. The parking was free because she'd been there for less than fifteen minutes, having rushed to get there after I texted to say my flight arrived early. I smiled at the familiar sights of my hometown as we drove down the wide, straight Memorial Avenue. The nicest part of travelling is coming home again.

"How was your dad?" asked Stef, looking across at me. I wished she would keep her eyes on the road.

"I don't know. I didn't see him much. He worked late most nights, most weekends and twice he went away on business trips. It was as if he were avoiding me or something."

"Why would he do that? You're his daughter! He invited you over and paid for your flight, didn't he?"

"Yes, but once I was there, he didn't seem to want to spend much time with me."

"So you didn't have a proper sit-down father-daughter talk, then?"

"No. We had a pizza together one night while he watched the rugby league on Sky Sports. And I gave him phone messages that I took when he was out. That was about it."

"Weird."

I contemplated this for a couple of minutes before my thoughts turned briefly to my mother. I hadn't seen her for ages. Perhaps I should make the effort to visit her in the hospital soon.

I noticed Stef missed the turn-off to our house in Riccarton and continued driving east.

I shot a glance at her. "Where are you taking us, Stef?"

She smiled at me. "To our new house, of course. I thought you'd want to get straight home."

"What new house? I don't know anything about a new house. What happened to our old house?"

"Oh, don't you know? Robert was supposed to text you. Or maybe that was me. One of us was going to, anyway, but I didn't."

"Never mind that," I said, fiddling with the rings in my ear, something I often do when something unexpected happens. "Just tell me what's going on. How and when and why did we have to move out of Matipo Street?"

"The landlord told us we had to leave. He's had enough of the earthquake and the aftershocks, and he's going to move to Brisbane. He decided to put all his rental places on the market at knock-down prices, and our house got bought while you were in Australia visiting your dad. We moved out yesterday."

"So where are we living now?" I asked. How strange it felt, coming home and not knowing where I lived anymore. It was dizzying and quite surreal.

"We've found a house in Avonside," said Stef.

"Avonside? That's nowhere near uni!" I protested. My heart palpitated at the abruptness of it all.

"I know. Sorry. But uni starts next week, and all the good houses anywhere near uni have been taken."

"What about the bad houses near uni?"

"Eh? No, there wasn't anything near uni at all. That's what I meant."

"So we're now on the other side of town? How are we

going to make that work?"

"Well, just look at it this way," said Stef. "We didn't have any choice. If you want to try to find a house closer to uni, go ahead. I'm telling you there's none available."

"Right. And has Robert figured out how he and I are going to get to uni every day?"

"The Orbiter. The bus route passes nearby and goes to uni, so you'll both be fine."

I was silent. I'd forgotten about that. It would have to do, obviously, but it wasn't as convenient as being walking distance from the university, like our old house in Matipo Street that we'd rented for almost a year. Inside, I squirmed while my fried brain tried to process all this unexpected information.

Stef also remained quiet while she drove The Frog through a particularly tricky roundabout without appreciably slowing down. The Frog had been known to stall on roundabouts in the past. It didn't like first or second gear very much, but it kind of tolerated third.

"We've moved all your stuff, Chloe, so don't worry about that," she said, once we were safely on the main road again. "I left Robert sorting out your room when I came to pick you up. You know how he likes organising stuff."

"He'll put everything in the wrong place!" Despite the fact that Robert was my boyfriend and we lived in the same house, we kept separate rooms, just sleeping with each other sometimes. We'd both decided that we each needed our own space a lot of the time, so this arrangement worked for us.

"He couldn't resist unpacking your books onto the bookcase. He's probably sorting them alphabetically." Stef grinned.

"I'll have to redo it," I complained. This kind of thing was often happening. Every morning, there was a dispute over where to put the food and drink in the refrigerator. We each have our own ideas about how to arrange things, and we don't always agree. That's normal when there are two Aspies in the same house. We spend a lot of time reorganising things that the other has arranged according to their own preference, to their utter indignation.

Stef drove over the edge of the kerb before bringing The Frog to a stop with a screech of brakes and a ghastly mechanical shuddering. Leafy trees lined the street, providing lots of shade for parked cars and pedestrians. We'd passed a large park about two or three blocks back that looked like a pleasant place for picnics or to take my laptop to update my blog. It seemed like a nice area. I turned to face the house in front of which Stef had parked.

It was an old two-storey brick house. I surveyed it for earthquake damage but couldn't see anything major. The chimney was still attached to the house, unlike many in Christchurch that had crashed to the ground during the earthquake last September. A small brick wall at the front boundary of the house had partially collapsed, but that was all the damage I could see.

I'd calmed down somewhat by now. "Looks great, but I wish you'd told me about it. It's a shock to come home and find home isn't where it used to be. You should've texted me."

"We've had this conversation already. I forgot, okay? You're lucky I remembered to come and pick you up from the airport. Everyone's still rattled and disorganised after the earthquake, remember? It's only been just over four months. The landlord didn't give us much notice to get out, either, the bastard. And while you've been away on holiday in Australia, we've had hundreds more aftershocks, and every time I worry that it might actually be the start of another big one. I just forgot to tell you about moving house, okay?"

Stef made a choking sound, then a soft sobbing. I turned to look at her, and saw her raise her right hand to her face. I stared, trying to determine if she was crying. It looked as if she was about to cry, but she stopped herself. Perhaps she was okay after all. Maybe it was just a loose eyelash irritating her eye. I hate it when that happens. I returned my attention to the property and surveyed the mature garden with a nod of appreciation.

"You're lucky I remembered to pick you up, Chloe," repeated Stef as if she'd already forgotten that she'd told me that. She wiped her eyes with a tissue. They were a little red.

"Didn't you write it in your diary?"

"Yes. I mean, I've been distracted by the aftershocks and having to move house. I don't even know where my diary is at the moment. Still packed in a box somewhere, I guess."

I was silent while I thought about this. The aftershocks bothered me, too, but during my few weeks away, I'd firmly put them out of my mind. Forgotten them. But of course my friends were getting reminders of 'the big one' several times a day.

"Is that why you're a bit tetchy, Stef?"

Stef made an expression that I couldn't properly interpret. It was a kind of grimace. "Yes, Chloe, it is."

I got out of the car and swung the door shut with a brutal clunk (it's the only way it will close). While I waited for Stef to get out and unlock the boot so I could pull out my bags, I looked carefully at the partially collapsed wall at the front of the property. A few loose bricks lay on the footpath against the side of the wall where someone had kicked them out of the way. A maze of cracks and small molehill-like mounds riddled the footpath where liquifaction had pushed up the asphalt but not broken through.

The car boot clicked open. Stef grabbed one of my bags, and I grabbed the other.

"Let's go in," she said, gesturing towards a gate that hung lopsidedly on one hinge. It didn't matter that it was broken because it probably wouldn't close anyway. Many gates and doors in Christchurch no longer shut properly as everything had been jostled about like hailstones bouncing off paving tiles by the earthquake and the interminable aftershocks.

I followed her towards the gate, but we both stopped, alarmed, at the sound of yelling and banging coming from the house next door. Its front door opened and slammed shut twice, as first one, then another, person came out in the midst of a fiery argument. The man, tall, gangly and bearded, jumped into a large derelict car parked on the front lawn and revved up the engine so much that I could barely make out the exact obscenities they used. Finally, he skidded the car off the lawn onto the driveway, swerved it out onto the road with a screech of tyres and a spray of gravel, and powered off down the road, glowering at us as he went past. The other person, a young woman armed with a fish knife (and half a flounder), stood in the road, shouting vehemently after him and gesturing angrily with the knife (and the fish), even after he had turned the corner. Then she glared at us as if we were somehow to blame for all her problems, if not the dire state of the world at large, and returned to her house, slamming the door closed behind her so hard the house reverberated.

Silence descended. From somewhere farther down the road, a dog snarled and barked as if in protest about the noise bombardment from the angry couple, but too late, because they'd both gone.

"Um, that's the neighbours," said Stef.

"Are they always like that?" I asked before I remembered that she and Robert had only taken possession of the house yesterday.

"Yeah, so far," sighed Stef. "But if you think that's bad, you should hear their kids."

We went inside, placed my bags against the side of the hall, and then Stef led me into the kitchen. I looked around, running my gaze around the perimeters of the floor, the table, and the cupboards, taking the measure of the place, drinking in every detail like fine wine. Actually, it was more like '70's Chateau Cardboard. The '70's décor looked dated and faded, certainly not to my taste, but it was tidy and clean. I hurried into the living room and surveyed that in the same manner. Again, it was satisfactory, though I felt uneasy because it was all unfamiliar to me. I rushed around the whole of the ground floor, checking out each room, poking my head into each cupboard, trying to familiarise myself with these parts of the house at fast-forward speed.

I heard Stef come up behind me and say something that I didn't catch, and I turned around.

"What?"

"I said, 'slow down'—I can see you're getting a bit uptight about this, Chloe. Breathe slowly and deeply. Just relax a bit. You'll get used to the house. It's actually quite nice once you've got used to the bright colours and flowery wallpaper. It's spacious too. I'm sure you'll like your room. You can't hear our rowdy neighbours from there unless they're in the back garden."

I gasped. I'd been so intensely focussed on investigating the ground floor living areas that I hadn't even thought about the bedrooms. I felt compelled to see those immediately, so, ignoring Stef's sensible advice, I rushed up the wooden bannistered stairs two at a time and paused on the landing, looking around. A yellow Post-it note was stuck to one of the doors, and I strode towards it. I recognised Stef's barely legible scrawl. She had written my name on the note with a pink highlighter pen.

I opened the door gingerly and went in, and I found Robert in there, sorting through boxes of my things. Robert is my boyfriend, and I hadn't seen him for four weeks because of my trip to Australia to see my dad—a visit that was a mostly a waste of time—but, right now, I wanted to investigate my new room.

"Hi." I barely glanced at him before turning my attention to the room in front of me, looking everywhere at once, rapidly sucking an impression of its size and shape into my head.

He looked up. "Hi," he said. "I missed you."

"Me, too." In some part of my mind, I wondered if he was smiling, demonstrating that he was overjoyed by my return, but all my attention was taken up looking around the room in which I would live for the foreseeable future. I scanned it, studying every aspect of it in detail: an old, worn, creaky-looking double bed; a battered chest of drawers, an old, white-painted bookcase. On the floor were several boxes, some closed, some opened. All of the opened ones contained books. They surrounded Robert and the bookcase like a conductor encircled by the front row of his orchestra. He would have to step over them to get out.

"Why are you home so soon?" asked Robert. I heard him clunking books into the bookcase, then reordering them, while I opened and examined each drawer of the bureau.

"My flight landed half an hour early." I turned to face him. My bureau investigation was completed. The drawers were all empty.

"Oh. Okay." Clunk. Another book went onto the bookcase.

"Aren't you pleased to see me?" I'm sure that he was, but now that I'd finished examining my room, I wanted him to say so.

The corners of his mouth turned down a little. I noticed how much his eye contact had improved over the past year since I first met him. His expression was unreadable to me, though. I started twirling the blue patch at the front of my hair, a self-soothing habit of mine. Twirling my hair is one of the ways I stim.

"No, not really," he admitted, "or, at least, not yet. I haven't finished unpacking your stuff. It was supposed to be a surprise for you when you got home. I wanted to finish this before you got here. Then I'd be pleased to see you."

"It doesn't matter about the unpacking. I want to unpack my own things anyway because you won't know where to put them. Give me a kiss." I smiled at Robert and moved towards him, intending to give him a hug, but the boxes in the way thwarted me. I reached over them, and so did he, and we met in the middle for a teetering cuddle and kiss above a box filled with psychology textbooks, books on Asperger's Syndrome and old *Star Trek: Deep Space Nine* DVDs.

"I'm happy that you're back," said Robert, pulling apart from me.

"Do you notice anything different about me, Robert?"

He appraised me studiously. "You've dyed some of your hair black."

"It's naturally black, silly. I've redone it with just a patch of blue."

"That's cool," he nodded. "This house doesn't feel like home yet. Has Stef told you about the neighbours?"

"Yes. I saw and heard them when we arrived. The adults, anyway. Stef said the kids are worse than them."

"Yeah, they are. I think there are only two of them now. The police took away one of the teenagers yesterday afternoon."

There was a welcoming meow from the floor near my leg, and I looked down. Our cat, Sex, rubbed my leg, clearly pleased to see me. I bent down to stroke her gently, and she purred with appreciation. I stood up abruptly, and she jumped into one of the boxes emptied of books, rattled around in it for a few moments and stuck her head out, askew, with a foxy look and another meow that made me laugh at her *cuteability*.

I peered past Robert to examine the contents of the bookcase more closely. Robert had unpacked about half of my books and put them on the shelves in a highly idiosyncratic way. I could see a psychology textbook next to a fantasy omnibus, for instance. Then I realised what he was doing and sighed.

"Robert, you can't order my books by size. That's ridiculous. How am I meant to find any particular book? You can't expect me to remember what format and size it is. I'm going to have to redo all of this myself."

"Wait. This isn't the final ordering. I was just doing it like this for fun. When I've unpacked them all, I'll reorder them by genre, sub-genre, and author. Wait and see."

"Well, okay... but I still think I should do it myself. Please move two of these boxes so I can get past, then I'll take over."

"No, Chloe, I'll do it," argued Robert, rocking backwards and forwards on his toes. He loved to arrange and rearrange books on bookshelves. He usually rearranged his own books at least once a month, sometimes taking them out and putting them back in exactly the same places. I knew he was secretly thrilled to have the opportunity to sort through my collection. He'd probably been looking forward to doing that more than seeing me back home after my holiday.

However, I felt hesitant about letting anyone, even Robert, sort through my books one by one. They're too personal. Seeing and touching all of someone's books is a bit like fondling their underwear. Nevertheless, Robert took my brief silence as confirmation that I would allow him to finish composing the contents of my bookcase, and he reached down to retrieve a chunky paperback, *Lord Of The Rings*. He was arranging one book at a time, naturally.

"Why don't you unpack your clothes while I do this?" suggested Robert, probably in an attempt to divert me from interrupting him further. "I had to pack them for you before we moved house yesterday, but I know you're quite particular about where they go."

"Of course I am. You might categorise your clothes by type and colour, but I like mine arranged by what I'm going to wear each day. And I bet you haven't really noticed what that is. I do have a system, you know."

"I know. That's why I left them for you to unpack." He grinned and leaned over to give me another kiss, clinging onto a copy of *The Hobbit*. I kissed him, then went over to the boxes of clothes and started pulling out garments to organise into seven piles, one for each day of the week, which I would then place in their own drawers. Except, I noticed, the bureau in this room only had six drawers in it. I frowned and stimmed by repeatedly tapping my left foot on the floor, wondering how I would handle the problem of having one drawer too few. I wouldn't wear one set of clothes for two consecutive days, and nor did I want to go around naked on Sundays. I needed a seventh drawer.

Robert interrupted my thoughts. "Stef's going to get some pizza for us. I'm having my usual one. I suppose you want your usual one?"

"Yes, of course I do." *Why would I want anything else?*

"That's good, because she's probably already gone to get it."

The solution to the drawer problem came to me. "Robert, do you have a chest of drawers like this in your room?"

"Yes," he said, without breaking his book-sorting stride.

"Are you using all the drawers, or do you have an empty one?" He's probably got at least one empty, I thought. He doesn't own many clothes, and he doesn't sort them in the same way as me.

He paused before answering, and I realised that I had asked him two closed questions with conflicting answers. He answered me clearly, though. "I do have an empty one. Do you want to take it?"

"Yes, thanks."

"Sure."

I stepped into the hall and checked the other doors to see if they had any yellow Post-it notes on them, but they didn't. Robert must have already removed the note Stef would have put on his door. I opened the nearest door and recognised his things. He'd already meticulously unpacked everything and stacked all the folded-up boxes neatly on his bed. Gathered around them were a few books, pens, loose papers and random clothing.

I smiled. *He's covered up his bed, so it looks like it can't be slept in because he wants to sleep with me tonight. Horny devil. Never mind if I'm feeling jet-lagged from the flight home—he intends to get his rocks off.*

I opened the drawers of the chest one by one until I found an empty one, the third one down. I pulled it out entirely and took it back to my own room, where I laid it on the floor underneath my own bureau. It matched and fitted the space perfectly. I nodded with satisfaction. Now I had seven.

Now that I had solved that problem, I unpacked the first box of my clothes. There were eight small ones that were jammed full, three shoeboxes of shoes, and three other little boxes containing just one large item each; fourteen altogether. I worked fast, segregating the clothes into each drawer, one per day, in the order in which I would wear them, with Monday's clothes in the top drawer and Sunday's clothes in the drawer I'd put underneath the chest. I put the remaining clothes into a couple of large black bin bags that I keep for this purpose. I would store those in a corner, and every two weeks I would swap some of my clothes in the bureau with those in the black bags to reorganise my wardrobe, or, in this case, *drawrobe*, which is a particularly satisfying neologism because it's an anagram of 'wardrobe'.

Robert was still pedantically working through my collection of books. Several boxes, some full and some empty, were scattered over most of the floorspace, so I put my empty boxes onto the bed, scattering them all over it, in contrast to the precise stacking he had employed in his own room. With my side vision, I saw Robert pause and glance in my direction, but I ignored him and started to arrange my computer peripherals on the desk. A slight twitch had started in my left eye, and I rubbed at it fiercely in annoyance. I knew that this symptom of stress was because I'd come home to find that home isn't home anymore.

Stef called out from the hall, interrupting our methodical organising. "Pizza's here, you two love birds. Hope I'm not catching you at a bad moment." She popped her head around the door and sniggered, perhaps expecting to find us *in flagrante delicto*, but instead, we were on opposite sides of the room. I was crawling under the desk with a power cable, trying to find an electric socket into which I could plug my laptop, while Robert stood at the bookcase, leafing through a copy of *Pride and Prejudice with Zombies*.

"Ah, Stef," he said. "I hope you remembered to get the garlic bread."

Chapter Two

Decisions are hard for me to make. Each one generates a whole heap of stress because of the uncertainty about whether the choice I make is the 'right' one. It doesn't make any difference whether it's a trivial thing, like whether to buy a book token as a present from this or that store, or whether it's a significant thing, like whether to stay at university and get a degree or not. It doesn't make any difference whether it's personal, like which studs and rings to adorn myself with, or whether it's impersonal, like which plumber to call when the drains stink. It doesn't even matter if there's no 'wrong' choice. They all cause anxiety, make my stomach churn and my head spin until I am so figuratively disoriented that, out of desperation, I would trade my freewill for a script for life that I could follow unwaveringly, simply to eliminate the stress of uncertainty.

It's not only not knowing the eventual result that causes the anxiety, either. It's the process of making the decision in the first place. I feel compelled to enumerate every possible outcome in my head, and all the possible direct and indirect effects of each of them. I guess everyone does this to some extent, but for me, it kick-starts a chain of negative thoughts. What if I make the wrong choice? What if I upset someone with my choice? It's daunting and gruelling struggling through this, like wading across a river of golden syrup, of which you cannot see the other side.

It is so much simpler not to make decisions at all, whenever possible. I have a set schedule detailing what I will wear each day of the week—it saves time, saves hassle and reduces anxiety, because I don't have to make the choice of what to wear when I'm still half-asleep. If I eat out, I'll always buy the same thing from a particular place. Why would I want something else, anyway? Why change, just for the sake of it? Better to stick with the same choice each time.

I had a horrible experience, years ago, that made me realise I needed to do this. I walked into a sandwich shop once that had one hundred and seventy-five varieties of packaged sandwiches. Of course, I had to look at all of them so I could make the best choice. It took twenty minutes to do just that. Then, I had to assess all of them, which is about as complex as deciphering a New York subway map, but with hunger pangs. In fact, it's almost impossible, as the human brain can only consider up to seven things at any one time. In my mind, I divided the sandwiches into groups by cabinet and row so I could determine the best choice in each group, then created subgroups from these selections, and evaluated those, then ascertained which was the best one of my preferred choices. By the time I'd done this, someone else had bought my choice, and I couldn't be bothered doing the whole evaluation again, so I left, hungry.

From then on, I decided this would not happen again. Painstakingly, I made a mental list of all the places from which I buy food, and the one thing from each place that I like the most. I only ever buy my preferred item from each place, and if they don't have it, then I have to go elsewhere, because buying a substitute item would upset the whole system. I then constructed a set of mental rules to follow to determine which place I would buy food from on any given day. That sometimes means I have to go out of my way to *get it, but that's easier than trying to decide out of so many alternatives.*

The pizza was scrumptious, just as good as I remembered it, which is, of course, exactly the way I want it to be. Stef's latest boyfriend, Phil, joined us, and we sat drinking wine and eating pizza for ninety-four minutes. At that time, I noticed that Robert had gone. I talked a little longer with Stef and Phil, another fourteen minutes actually, before they excused themselves, and said they wanted 'to have an early night'. He he. I've worked out what that means.

I went looking for Robert and found him in my bedroom. He'd finished arranging my books properly and was standing back, admiring his work. I took a cursory glance at them and could see that he'd put them all back in exactly the same order I had them at the old house. I nodded, almost imperceptibly, in recognition of his achievement, but he totally missed this. Instead, he watched Sex happily playing, jumping in and out of some of the empty boxes.

I felt tired and restless at the same time. Aeroplane journeys always have that effect on me, and I get into a 'kind of want to sleep but know that I bloody well won't be able to' mood. The dinner I'd eaten had not been any help: two-thirds of a large salami-topped pizza and five glasses of wine that, instead of inducing sleepiness, had made me feel bloated. It all seemed to sit in my stomach like cold, greasy porridge—the lumpy kind—and made me fart like a hippopotamus whenever I giggled, which I did a lot, because of the wine. I even felt a little nauseated. Probably *wine flu*. I certainly didn't want to go to bed feeling like that.

"Wanna go out to a café?" asked Robert. He looked at his watch. "Nine-twenty-three p.m. That's not too late for a drink."

I frowned. I knew all of the cafés local to our old house in Riccarton, but I wasn't familiar with this area at all. That was another thing I knew I'd have to adjust to. "I don't know anywhere around here. I don't know this part of town. Why couldn't you and Stef find somewhere much nearer to the university? Oh, don't answer. That was a rhetorical question. She explained it to me already anyway. Do you know somewhere we can go for a green tea?"

"No. We only moved here yesterday, Chloe. But every area has cafés. If we walk to the local shops, we'll probably find one."

"Okay, Robert, let's go. You lead the way."

I grabbed my sweatshirt and bag, which I'd thrown on the floor by the bed, followed Robert out into the hall and waited at the top of the stairs while he fetched his own bag. I wouldn't be ready for sleep for some time; although I felt tired, my mind constantly prickled as if jolted by static electricity, trying to process the myriad of changes. I knew it would take me a while to settle into a new house. I thought that if I'm not going to be able to sleep, I may as well do something fun.

We left the house and walked swiftly along the dark suburban street, the heels of my boots clicking sharply on the pavement in contrast to Robert's trainers, which made almost no sound. An occasional car drove by. The street was dimly-lit, and the late evening air was mild as it was late summer. The smell of long grass and algae wafted from the river on the other side of the road. We walked for a block, turned a corner, and walked another two blocks before Robert paused at the next intersection.

I had an uneasy feeling that he didn't know where he was going.

"Robert, do you actually know where the local shops are?"

"Well... no, I don't, but I thought we would find them easily enough. There must be some around here."

"So you've been walking around with no idea where you're going? Shit. I thought you were going to take us to a café."

"I will, when I find one. It was your idea that we go out, remember? I would've been happy to stay home."

"You suggested it. I only agreed because I thought you knew where we were going."

I looked in all directions, squinting because we stood under a corner street light and the glare hurt my eyes. The quiet of the night was interrupted by a low rumble and the gentle roll of a minor aftershock, the third I'd felt since I got home that day. It felt like a 3.2 or something out west. Nothing to be concerned about.

"It looks like there might be some shops that way." I pointed towards what appeared to be a main road a block over. I knew that shops usually congregated on the main roads. I didn't know whether there actually were any on that main road, on the stretch nearest to us, but it seemed to be our best chance.

We walked there. There was a slight breeze in the air, but it was still mild. I was warm enough because we walked quickly, and the glasses of wine I'd had kept the chill out. Unfortunately, they also made me want to pee. *Geez, we had better find a café around the corner, or I'm going to become uncomfortable before long.*

Luckily for us, there was a small group of shops just around the corner, and they did have a café, but its windows were dark. It was obviously closed, but we went over to check it anyway, just to be sure.

Robert peered at the opening times etched on the door. "Closes at four p.m," he said. He stared through the glass door as if affronted, but his voice was level and even, or at least I thought it was. I joined him at the door and peered through. We couldn't even make out anything inside, it was so murky.

"Great," I said.

"Why's that great?"

"No, it's not great, Robert." I wriggled uncomfortably. The coolness of the breeze seemed to encourage the call of nature even more.

"I'm confused. Why did you say it's great that the café's closed?"

"I was being sarcastic. I've explained this to you, remember? I meant the opposite of what I said. That's what people do when they want to emphasise that something really isn't the way they have just said it is. Do you get it?"

"No, but it's fine."

"Really?"

"No, now I was being sarcastic."

"Great, thanks."

"Was that more sarcasm, Chloe?"

I shook my head. I didn't even know myself. "More like *sarchasm*. With an 'H'."

"What do you mean?"

"The gulf between what I said and what you thought I meant."

"Oh. Right."

"Never mind. Let's walk on. I think I can see a service station up ahead. They might have toilets."

"I don't need to go to the toilet. Will they have coffee,

do you think?"

And green tea. "Let's find out. Come on." I walked off, grabbing Robert's shirtsleeve as I passed, almost pulling him off balance. He quickly fell into step beside me. I hurried on even faster, propelled by the mounting pressure in my full bladder.

Robert reached down and took my hand, squeezing it gently as we walked. "I'm so glad you're home with me," he said, swatting away some night flies with his other hand.

"We're not home," I retorted. I think I was feeling cross now, but maybe I was merely tired. I never quite know. "We're out god-knows-where in the dark, looking for a non-existent café."

"I meant I'm glad you're back in Christchurch." Another hand squeeze.

"Yeah, me too," I relented. *About fifty metres to the service station. Can I hold on long enough?*

The bright lights of the service station forecourt burned like a beacon, and we, like moths drawn inexorably to a lamp in a dark room, approached. It was quiet. A young Asian woman at the counter looked up as we entered, put her iPod down and stood. "Can I help you?" she said.

"I'll have a trim latté," said Robert.

"Awesome," replied the woman. "And for you?" she said, looking at me.

"A toilet," I blurted. "Have you got a toilet here?"

The woman nodded. "Behind you."

I turned and made my way there urgently. "Order me the usual," I called to Robert over my shoulder.

He was waiting with a single hot drink when I re-emerged, feeling much better. It was nine-fifty-eight now, though it felt earlier than that to me as my body clock was still on Melbourne time, but all the wine had gone to my head, and I hoped the green tea would start to clear it.

"Sorry, Chloe," said Robert, sipping from the takeaway cup. "They've run out of green tea here. Do you want a coffee instead? It's good."

"No. I don't drink coffee."

"I know. Maybe you should take it up." Robert sighed and gulped more of his drink. I turned to the young woman behind the counter. She was gathering receipts from the till, but stopped and smiled at me, shaking her head from side to side.

"Sorry, we've run out of green tea. But we do awesome coffee. Would you like one? I'm closing at ten, but I can make you one, no trouble."

"No, I don't drink coffee." My voice came out as a strained whisper. I felt irritated. I'd just had almost the same exchange of words with Robert, and I find it downright annoying to have to repeat what I've just said. I glanced at the clock on the wall. Nine fifty-nine.

"Sorry, I didn't hear you. Please say it again."

A threepeat. Even worse. "I don't drink coffee," I snapped. There wasn't much time left until closing. "Do you have English Breakfast tea?"

"Yes. With milk?" The woman's voice had dropped a little, and she had crossed her arms. Her smile had gone. Perhaps something I'd said or done had *unsmiled* her.

"I'll have one with milk, please," I said, in the friendliest voice I could muster. That'll have to do, and just in time. It was still not yet ten o'clock, and I'd ordered. She'll have to make the drink now.

The woman busied herself at the hot drinks station. Robert slurped his coffee, waiting by the door. I tapped my right foot on the floor as I stared at the clock, as if by doing so I could somehow freeze time. It didn't work. The clock ticked over to ten o'clock.

"Oh, awesome! I've found some green tea. It was hidden behind the chai latte." The woman turned and held up a small box on which I couldn't read the label because she had her hand over it. "Would you still like a green tea?"

I felt truly annoyed now. "Yes, I would, but it's too late," I groaned. "I ordered the English Breakfast tea before ten o'clock."

"It's no trouble. I can make you a green tea if you want it."

"You can't take new orders after closing time," I persevered. I fiddled with the rings in my right ear. The muscles in my face and arms had tightened with stress.

"Do you want the English Breakfast, then?"

"No, I don't want English Breakfast tea when you've got green tea!"

The woman looked at me with an expression I didn't recognise. "I don't understand."

"It's too late for me to order the green tea now," I complained and, in a sudden huff brought on because she misunderstood my irrational logic, or simply as a side effect of too much wine and stress, I headed past Robert and bustled through the door.

He followed. "It's a pity the service station closed before you could get your drink, but I think the woman wanted to make you one anyway."

I didn't reply. I felt too upset. A new house in a new area to deal with, and here I was, wandering around the dark streets, unable even to buy a green tea before the only place open closed.

We walked quickly in the direction from which we had come. The night air was pleasantly mild at this time of year. I stared at the night sky, looking for patterns amongst the stars that had re-emerged now we were some distance from the bright lights of the service station. The night air and the starlit tranquillity brought me some peace, but I still felt light-headed from the wine.

Robert discarded his takeaway cup as we passed a rubbish bin at a bus stop.

"Was the coffee good?" I asked.

"It was awesome," he said, parodying the woman at the service station, then grinned at me. I smiled and gave him a playful punch in the arm, giggling. It felt good to be with him again.

We walked towards home slowly. Robert put his free hand around my shoulders and pulled me closer. He does that sometimes because he's seen other couples walking like that. When we were first dating and he touched me like that, I would pull away from him because his hand pressure was too soft and it felt irritating to me, like a fly settling on bare skin. But we worked out that he simply needed to apply more pressure, and by doing so, create a reassuring physical contact. Deep pressure is calming for me; light pressure is stimulating and unpleasant.

We reached our street. At least, I think it was our street, but I honestly couldn't be certain at first, because of the dimness and its unfamiliarity. Eventually, the unmistakable outline of The Frog parked at the side of the road with one front wheel on the kerb emerged from the gloom. We were almost home.

Robert gave me a couple of shoulder squeezes and said, "Do you need your own space after your trip back, Chloe? Or shall we sleep together tonight and make love?"

I knew this was coming, and of course I wanted to spend the night with him. *Silly thing. Why would he think differently?* I laughed, partly because of the situation, but mostly because of the wine. I was a little *fuzzled.*

"And how are we going to do that?" I said, poking him playfully in the ribs. "Both our beds are covered with boxes."

"We can move those, obviously," he said, frowning.

"I'm horny already," I teased and smooched Robert on the cheek. "It's been weeks since we've been together. Do you really want to wait while we tidy up? That's not very romantic."

We passed under one of the street lamps, and in its harsh light I could see Robert's clenched jaw and slightly flushed face. I knew this was a dilemma for him because he didn't know what to say, and I enjoyed that in a mischievous way. I giggled again. I felt flushed too, but it was probably because of the wine.

"Um..." was Robert's unequivocally vague and useless response.

"How about we snuggle down and get busy on one of the sofas?" I suggested playfully, poking him again. It wouldn't be the first time they've been used for that purpose. Or the second.

"No, Chloe. What if Stef and her boyfriend come downstairs and find us in the middle of passionate lovemaking?"

I tittered. "Could be embarrassing," I admitted. "Um hmm, so what are we going to do?"

"Besides," continued Robert, "those old sofas are horrible even to sit on, with their thin foam cushions and their worn, uneven springs. We would probably be less uncomfortable in a tree."

I laughed out loud. The dog farther down the street barked agitatedly as if joining in with his own comments on the matter. We walked a few more paces and were almost home now.

"What a great idea," I said. "Let's do it. It'll be fun. I want to do it outside sometime, you know, be one with nature and all that. Be a hippie for a while. Live on the edge."

"The edge of what?"

"I mean, be adventurous. Take risks. Try new things. Seize the moment. Embrace the glorious absurdity of the situation. Embrace each other up a tree."

"You've had far too much wine," admonished Robert.

I knew that was true. It had made me giggle and spout nonsense, yet in some kind of *alcohological* way, it all seemed to make sense to me.

"That one will do." I pointed to a large oak tree by the side of the river, almost opposite our house. "Some of the boughs are easy to reach from the ground, and they appear solid enough. We could get up there easily."

"You're serious!" Robert laughed now, quietly, because typically he was too self-conscious to laugh loudly.

"Yes, why ever not? Let's go out on a limb for a change. I mean literally. Just this one *oak-casion*."

"What *acorny* joke," he rebutted.

"Oh, come on, Robert. Let's see what's it's like. It might be *tree-mendous*." I smirked. "We'll be warm enough. No one's going to know. It's late. Even the ducks are asleep."

I slipped out of Robert's hold, catching his hand as it fell away from my shoulders, and set off across the road to the riverbank, pulling him along behind me. He'd had a couple of glasses of wine with me earlier too, and didn't put up much resistance to me leading the way. I went over to the oak tree I'd chosen. It had a wide, sweeping, low bough ideal for our purposes.

I pulled myself up onto the bough, sat astride it and shuffled along. It curved around behind the tree, away from the road and the houses. With the river on this side, the tree trunk would almost perfectly hide us from view.

Robert hesitated for a few moments, then swung himself up onto the tree limb and edged along behind me.

"I can't believe I'm doing this," he muttered, which made me laugh. I thought it was fun. Or maybe that was the wine thinking. I don't know, really.

I reached a point where the bough forked into two narrower limbs that snaked together horizontally for a short distance before diverging and rising. This spot looked perfect for what I had in mind, and I lay back on the twinned limbs and waited for Robert to catch up.

"You're totally mad, you know," he said. "I don't think any other woman could have enticed me to do this crazy stunt."

I gave him a sharp look. *What other woman...! Oh, he's talking theoretically.*

Robert looked around, holding onto the bough to maintain his balance. "We probably can't be seen from the road in this spot, in the dark. Well, Chloe, what next?"

To answer him, I grabbed his sweatshirt, pulled him closer and kissed him passionately on the lips. Quickly, I pulled off his sweatshirt and my own, and tucked them behind and underneath us on the tree boughs, creating a thin, padded layer as a kind of bed. Or a nest. I'm not sure what to call it. But it was kind of snug and cosy.

We kissed again. I had been away in Australia for several weeks, so we hadn't had the opportunity for close physical contact like this for some time, and I had missed it. A lot. Our kissing deepened; I began to realise just how much I'd been missing it, and how *redonculous* a situation I'd got us into. Instead of us snuggling up in bed together, reminding each other of just how much we loved to be together physically, here we were, at my own freakish suggestion, up a tree on the riverside, cuddling and hanging on to the foliage instead of to each other so we wouldn't fall out.

It was exciting though, despite the precariousness of our position. Robert was getting into it now. He moved a little closer, almost lying on me. Our passion increased, and the tree limbs began to sway gently with a soft swishing sound. I pulled him even nearer. He undid the buttons on my jeans and then loosened his, while I tried to shuffle mine off my waist.

I hugged him tightly as we moved together in physical harmony, our own sounds chorused by the swishing of the leafy branches around us. This was much more fun that I'd expected, and I no longer minded that we weren't safe at home in a warm bed right now. Somehow, the excitement of this bizarre situation enhanced the experience for me. The amount of sway we had in the tree was phenomenal. It was as if the earth was moving.

Then I realised that it actually was moving. Yet another of the incessant aftershocks had started. The ground emitted a loud crack, followed by a deep rumbling sound. Above us, small branches whipped back and forth, and the pair of boughs on which we reclined jerked rather than swayed.

"Aftershock!" said Robert, trying to get a better grip on the tree and me at the same time.

Over his shoulder, a tiny light caught my eye. A lit cigarette. I realised someone was standing across the road, outside our neighbour's house, smoking. Possibly watching us. I didn't know if he could see us or not.

We lost our balance and tumbled from the tree. I barely had time to open my mouth to scream before we hit the water together, making an enormous splash. I swallowed a mouthful of the foul river water, cold and slimy. I tried to suppress the thought that it was probably full of duck shit and eel pee, but I couldn't. I gagged. My bottom plonked on the riverbed, with Robert on top of me, squeezing the air out of my lungs. I felt my unfastened jeans being pulled off my legs by the current and tried to hook them with one foot, but failed.

Robert stood on my leg as he tried to get his footing, and I took in another mouthful of water. Then I felt his hand on my arm. He pulled me upright. We stood in about half a metre of water. I could feel stuff in my hair and didn't want to touch it to find out what it was. I vehemently spat out the water in my mouth.

"Fuck! That's horrible!"

"The aftershock's over. I think that was probably a four, at least. What do you think, Chloe?"

I stared at him. Yes, we usually did try to estimate the magnitude and depth and approximate location of the aftershocks (and after thousands of them, we were good at it), but I didn't feel like doing that right now. I was cold, wet, slimy and half-naked. I realised our sweatshirts had gone downstream in the current along with my jeans.

"Are you all right?" asked Robert. He waded towards the riverbank, leaving me in the water. He had somehow managed to keep his jeans on, and was fumbling to do them up.

"I'm all right," I said. Now the shock had passed, the hilarity of the situation hit me, and I laughed uncontrollably. Robert stopped, turned back to face me, and cracked a broad grin. He reached out a hand for me, and I took it. He pulled me towards the bank while I laughed like some fish out of one of Dr Seuss's wacky children's books. I trudged across the muddy river bottom and realised one of my boots had gone, too.

I reached the edge and tried to scramble up the bank, but it was too steep and slippery. I felt Robert behind me, pushing on my bum as I tried to pull myself up. From nowhere, a little orange light appeared, and a large, brawny hand reached down to grab mine. Seconds later, I was hauled up onto the bank, where I stood dripping, half-naked and shivering, staring into the grinning face of the man who had scowled at us from his car earlier that day—my new neighbour—but he didn't comment on that at all.

"Welcome to Avonside," he said. "I reckon that one was a four point two, maybe ten kilometres deep."

Chapter Three

Robert asked me once why I'm studying psychology instead of computer science. He said he had noticed I'm good with computers, which is true, and I'm probably not good at psychology because I dropped out in the first year. I told him that it wouldn't have mattered what subjects I did in my first year, I would have dropped out anyway as I had such a torrid time struggling with my emergence into womanhood, my Asperger's diagnosis, my bipolar disorder diagnosis and the various other, possibly wrong, diagnoses, or should that be diagnosi, so much so that I was overwhelmed with not knowing who or what I was. Ironically, getting through that difficult time in my life may have kindled and enhanced my interest in psychology.

Sure, I have an affinity with computers. I can throw a website together in a couple of hours, hack into social media sites to annoy people, infiltrate local pizza delivery websites to get free pizzas, and write computer programs in seven languages. But computers are just a tool to me. Other than getting them to do what I want (and quickly, because I'm not patient), I've no interest in them.

I don't understand people, though. And that includes myself, but I especially mean other, Non-Spectrum, people. They are enigmas, tantalising perplexities that I just want to categorise and unravel and break down into tiny comprehensible psychological chunks to see if there is even an iota of sense to be found.

That's what makes psychology so fascinating: trying to understand why people are the way they are, and why they do the things that they do in the way that they do them, because I don't do those things in the same way, or at all, if you see what I mean. And while I genuinely don't understand the motives behind why other people do those things, and I don't share them, I can detect patterns in their words and actions. I can define them, categorise and subcategorise them into some logical and consistent structure in my mind. It's just one more step to go from that to understand the psychology behind it all, at least in my mind, anyway.

So, maybe that's the reason I am studying psychology. It's a journey into the unknown, for me, trying to figure out what's going on in other people's heads. Being an Aspie (that's what those of us with Asperger's Syndrome call ourselves), that's what I have to do all the time anyway. In fact, I put a lot of effort into trying to understand other people, whereas NS (Non-Spectrum) people usually don't have to do that because it is quite natural for them to notice and comprehend all the non-verbal communication. Most of the time, most NS people understand most other NS people, and they don't have to work at it with the same intensity that I have to. And because they don't have to work at it, and their perception and understanding of others is usually right, they don't realise so readily when their perception or understanding is wrong. Whereas I know that most of the time, my perception and understanding of others is wrong, and I'm genuinely surprised when it isn't, and I learn something from that.

University started again. It was my third year, though I was only taking second year subjects in the main because I flunked out atrociously in my first year and had to repeat most of it. It was Robert's second year. He continued with Economics, while I kept on with Psychology and a mishmash of other subjects, aiming towards an Arts degree and, maybe, some idea of what I might do when I graduate.

We were used to the student lifestyle, eating cheaply, buying second-hand clothes, trying to scrape by on a meagre student allowance. We had continued doing this, even after Robert and I won a pile of money on a foreign exchange trade he'd forgotten about last year, but that's another story, and it's in his own diary, and I can't tell it anyway because I don't really understand any of that stuff at all. Robert spent all his share on university course fees, apart from a small amount he kept aside to dip into to pay for coffees and cakes. That's probably a good thing. He's clever, but I don't think he's clever with money. His win on the FX trade was probably down to luck rather than skill. I think that's why he hasn't tried to repeat it. I hung onto mine with the vague idea of investing it somehow, but I haven't done anything about that yet. That's probably a good thing too.

It was Tuesday, February 22nd, the second day of the first semester, another fine, hot day. I'd had a couple of lectures on the Monday, and there were two more today. The first of these had finished thirty-five minutes ago, and I had been into one of the cafés to have a green tea and a light lunch. Robert had a lecture on now, so we weren't able to meet to eat together.

To pass some time, I walked around the campus towards the university bookshop. It was more appealing at present to browse the latest speculative fiction novels in there for half an hour than doing the required reading for my courses. There's time for that later. I can't keep myself out of bookshops for long. I love looking through the new titles, scanning my favourite shelves to see which books have been added or taken out, and rearranging any that are out of place. Sometimes I just like to handle the books, sniff their 'new book' smell and flip through the pages. Other times I enjoy looking at the neat patterns they make stacked together on the shelves, or I like to count them or the number of different authors.

After browsing there for a while, I felt that I was ready to get started on my course reading, and I walked over to the library. I made my way to a table in a small niche area I knew about and presumably most other students hadn't found, because all of last year there were usually only two or three other students in my special spot. I didn't know them, but they were familiar strangers, and that's less uncomfortable than people I don't even recognise surrounding me. Only one of them was there today, a young woman scribbling furiously in her workbook.

I sat and pulled out a photocopy of *Unskilled and Unaware of It: How Difficulties in Recognising One's Own Incompetence Lead to Inflated Self-Assessments (Kruger & Dunning, 1999)*, an article I was supposed to read for Psychology. This actually sounded intriguing. I'd always wondered why losers and idiots think they're talented at everything.

I had barely read the first page when a loud rumbling sound began. I knew what that meant—it was another aftershock. This one abruptly became intensely worse than the usual ones. The growling of the earth increased to the volume of a jet engine as if the earth had tremendous hunger pangs and was about to open up and swallow everything in a cavernous, earthen mouth. The chair bucked and jolted beneath me violently, nearly throwing me off.

The familiar stranger next to me dropped to the ground in a crouching position and ducked under the desk. "Get down!" she cried, yanking my arm. I rolled off the bouncing chair onto the heaving floor and scrambled under the desk. The young woman was now busily texting into her mobile phone. "I'm so fucking sick of this," she said.

From my cover, I looked towards the tall glass windows. The panes seemed to vibrate, or that may have been the buildings and trees I could see swaying. Suddenly, I had an urge to get out of there and tried to scramble to my feet so I could bolt for the exit, but the quake had become too powerful for that, so I stayed on the floor under the desk, deafened by the grating, rumbling noise. I was scared now, but relieved that I wasn't in a high-rise car park building or in a supermarket with jars of marmalade and bottles of wine and packets of food flying everywhere. Instead, books were flying. Not far from me, books tumbled from their shelves, the sound of them crashing to the floor almost totally muffled by the cacophony from outside. In contrast, flakes of something floated down from the ceiling quietly and gently to settle like snowflakes on the floor and on the upturned volumes. From somewhere within the building came a woman's cry, much higher in pitch than the deep, gravelly grumble that roared from Mother Earth outside.

Though it felt as if it would never end, after thirty seconds or so the shaking slowed in intensity and eventually stopped, along with the rumbling noise, which ground down to nothing. But there was no sinister quietness like you see in B-grade movies after a disaster. There was pandemonium. People shouting, moving, running, all throughout the library. I could hear water gushing somewhere above me. I looked up but couldn't see any water, yet not knowing where it was scared me more. For the first time, I thought that I was lucky to be alive. The earthquake had definitely felt worse than the September one. And because it was lunchtime on a weekday, there would be more damage and injuries this time.

"Let's get out of here!" The young woman under the desk with me shook my shoulder violently, jerking me out of my maudlin thoughts and back into the nightmare reality we were in.

She and I stuffed our things into our bags and hurried outside to join a crowd of milling students. They swarmed out of the bookshop, the various cafés, the library, the lecture theatres; some were laughing, a few were crying, some sat on the steps with glazed-over eyes, but most of them were talking with unbridled excitement. I felt panicky now, not knowing what to do, afraid to leave, even to speak, least it all start happening again.

A man dashed up to me, grabbed my upper arms and shook me until I looked directly at him. I recognised him from my Psychology tutorial last year.

"Are you okay?" he demanded, right in my face.

"Yes," I said, so he would go away. He let go of my arms and moved off. I closed my eyes for a few moments, trying to block everything out because I felt overwhelmed and dizzy. People streamed past me, bumping into me. I vaguely remembered that we were supposed to go somewhere in the event of a major earthquake, but where?

I opened my eyes as some security people and lecturers came running towards us, shouting, "What the hell are you doing? Get away from the buildings! Assemble at the Ilam Fields!"

The Ilam Fields. Now I remembered that was the evacuation area. Rather than walk straight there, I went in the opposite direction. I knew where Robert's lecture was, and I wanted to find him, so we could go to the evacuation point together. He's calm in the aftershocks. They don't seem to bother him. They make me feel nauseated, though, and have ever since the first major one, when the bookcase in my room fell over beside my bed and almost crushed me.

Staff and students alike continued to stream out of the library, down the steps and past me. Many of them had their mobile phones in their hands, jabbing at the buttons, writing texts as they walked. I realised I could do the same and pulled my cell phone from my bag as I skirted the library and approached the octagonal lecture theatre building.

There were too many people coming out and milling around for me to locate Robert quickly. He might even walk past me in the crowd without us seeing each other, I realised. I tried to call him, but it was impossible. The cell phone network was overloaded, and I couldn't get through.

"Chloe!"

I looked up just as Robert reached my side. "I tried to call you," I said. "There's no network. How did you find me?"

"I saw your blue hair through the crowd."

Yes, of course. My distinctive cobalt blue dyed patch of hair makes me stand out in a crowd. He could easily spot me amongst the swarming students. I grabbed his arm. "We need to go to Ilam Fields. That's where everyone is going, I think. We're supposed to assemble there and wait for the all-clear."

"Okay," he replied, and we moved off. "That was a bad one, Chloe. Some of the ceiling tiles were shaken loose and came down on us."

"Anyone hurt?"

"Yes, I think so. The tiles are made of plaster, and they're heavy. The lecture theatre's a mess, too. Lectures will probably have to be called off for the rest of the day, maybe longer."

I fished in my bag for my beret and pulled it firmly onto my head. It was a tight fit, which is exactly what I needed. It's calming and cosy somehow. I've carried it with me every day since the September quake, and I wear it often. I can't bear to be without it.

Then we made our way towards Ilam Fields, along with hundreds of other students. I don't like crowds at all and generally avoid them whenever possible, especially if they are moving. You can never be sure they won't turn into a human stampede, but I believed this one wouldn't. It was an orderly evacuation, as we'd all become inured to the frequent aftershocks, and almost everyone was calmer now that the shock of it had passed. The 7.1 magnitude quake in the previous year had shaken me considerably, but now I could cope with them better. This one did seem worse than that, though.

On the Ilam Fields, students and staff congregated, some in large groups and some in smaller *grouplets*. Robert and I wandered amongst them. I felt restless, and I wondered if Robert felt the same, so I asked him. He said he did, and he wanted to walk around, as the physical effort helped relieve the anxiety of not knowing what was going to happen next.

My cell phone emitted the sound of the *Star Trek* transporter, and I jumped as I wasn't expecting it. The network must be working again. I glanced around as I pulled my phone out of my bag. A few of the other students appeared to be texting, but I hadn't noticed this, as I'd become so wrapped up in my own fretfulness.

It was a lengthy text from my dad. I read it and blanched.

"Shit. This is much worse than the September quake, Robert. Dad's watching it all unfold on the news in Melbourne. There are buildings down in the CBD, and the spire's fallen off the cathedral."

"What about the buildings in the CBD?" Robert looked at the ground while replying. I reasoned that he was struggling with his own inner thoughts, too distracted to pay full attention to what I was saying.

"Some of them are down. I mean, fallen down. People were killed, and many people may be missing."

"People were killed?"

"Yes, that's what they're reporting on Australian TV. Wait, Dad wants to know if I'm all right. He tried to call, but couldn't get through. Apparently, we're not supposed to be using the phone lines anyway, just texts, so emergency services can keep their communication lines open to operate."

"That's terrible."

It was my turn to be confused. For a moment, I thought he meant it was terrible that the phones weren't working, but then I realised he was talking about the dead people. And that reminded me that Dad was probably worried that I was one of them.

"Hang on, I better reply to Dad's text." Swiftly, I tapped out a short message saying that I was fine, and sent it.

"Have you heard from Stef?" said Robert abruptly. "She works in the CBD, doesn't she?"

My heart skipped a beat. My throat suddenly felt dry, and I swallowed. "I haven't heard from her. I'll text her. I hope she's all right. Why hasn't she contacted us?"

"Maybe she can't get a message through."

"What if she's not all right? We don't know one way or the other."

"The odds are that she's fine."

"But she might not be. We don't know." I heard myself talking faster and at a higher pitch, so I stopped talking. I tapped out a text message at warp speed and pressed 'send'. It took a while, but it seemed to go through. I'd no sooner stuffed my phone back into my bag when another text came through.

"Is that Stef?" asked Robert as I read the message.

"No, it's my auntie Eileen in New York. She's watching pictures of it on the news there. She wants to know if I'm okay. I'd better reply, I guess."

Robert's phone beeped. "My mum," he said, checking it. "She's fine, but her chimney fell down onto her car and wrecked it. Have you texted your mother, Chloe?"

"I can't text her, she doesn't have a cell phone. I can call the hospital, though." I tried, but I couldn't get through. Concerned relatives had probably overloaded their call system.

Around us, other phones beeped and rang as the students close by were contacted by their relatives and friends. We hung around, not sure what to do, surrounded by excited or frightened voices and the constant tap-tap-tap of people texting.

My phone alerted me to another text message, and I flipped it open quickly, hoping it was a message from Stef. It wasn't.

"Stef?" asked Robert.

"No. It's her mother—my auntie Ingrid. She wants to know if I've seen or heard from Stef. I'll just reply." I rapidly sent a response. It had misspellings, because my thumb couldn't text straight. I felt anxious about what might have happened to her, but Ingrid must have been frantic. She lived in Nelson, five hours' drive away, unable to do anything to locate her daughters except phone and text them incessantly.

"It was a six-point-three," said Robert. "I've just looked it up."

"Shit! It felt a lot worse than the September one, and that was a seven-point-one."

"Yeah, but it was only six kilometres deep, and much closer to the city. That's why the ground acceleration was much worse. Oh..."

"What?"

"It was in a different place to the others. It wasn't west, it was in the hills."

I dropped to the ground and sat there hugging my knees, rocking, trying to take this information in. I didn't remember the hills being on the fault line. Maybe this was a new fault line to the south? Maybe the damned earthquakes would never stop.

There was a sharp aftershock at that moment, accompanied by a deep rumbling and a distinct cracking sound. I could see cars bouncing off the surface of Ilam Road as they drove by. The university towers *quagswagged* like poplars in a breeze. I don't know if they actually did sway like that or not, but it looked like it. Someone nearby started to cry. Maybe a first-year student who didn't know anyone yet, or someone suffering from post-traumatic stress disorder after the September earthquake.

And I still hadn't heard from Stef.

"Let's go home," I said, getting up. "I want to go

home."

There seemed little or no chance of getting a bus home, so we walked. It was mid-afternoon by now. The streets were clogged with more traffic than I'd ever seen, so even if we had waited for a bus and one had come, it wouldn't have been quicker than walking anyway. It was as if everyone in Christchurch was trying to get somewhere.

We walked down the Fendalton Road and across the north side of Hagley Park. So far, we'd only seen a small amount of damage. Some buckled and cracked roads, a few collapsed walls. Lots of people walking the other way. Several small aftershocks of the rumbling and rolling kind punctuated our walk.

Dust clouds swirled above the central city in the distance, testament to unseen devastation there. Military helicopters flew in and out of the area, periodically filling the air with the sound of whirling chopper blades. Clearly, the inner city had been hit worse than the western suburbs.

I checked my phone. There were no new texts.

"I still haven't heard from Stef," I said. I felt anxious, sick even. It was not like her not to respond, especially after a large aftershock.

"Maybe the network's overloaded again," said Robert. "Or maybe her phone is out of charge."

He was quiet for a while after that. I didn't know if he was worried about Stef or not. I was, though.

The aftershocks continued, but with less intensity than before. I'd become so inured to them that they no longer disturbed me unless they were about a 'five' and, thankfully, those had been sporadic.

We reached Bealey Ave, one of the four main avenues

surrounding the CBD. I gasped and grabbed Robert's arm. Here, the earthquake had pummelled the old buildings on both sides of the tree-lined avenue. The façade of the Carlton Hotel had broken off and overhung the car park and footpath at a thirty-degree angle. The roof and stone walls of the old Knox church across the road had collapsed, scattering rubble all over the intersection with Victoria Street. Now it looked like an ancient Celtic ruin. These landmarks had been there all my life and for generations before, damaged beyond repair in a few seconds of tremendous upheaval.

It slowly dawned on me that Christchurch would never be the same again. *Quake City*. It deserves that name now. Quake City.

The army had closed or blocked off some of the roads, so we had to divert and walk a longer way around. Parts of Fitzgerald Ave looked impassable, and we tried to weave our way through the back streets of Richmond. It was after four-thirty now. We had to trudge through sludge several centimetres deep, as we got closer to home—the dreaded liquifaction, the muddy gunk forced up from underground during the earthquake. It ruined my shoes, but that didn't matter. I had another pair at home. I've read that some women have dozens of pairs of shoes, but I've never had more than three at a time.

The *Star Trek* transporter sound indicated that another text message had arrived. I flipped my cell phone open to read it.

"It's from Stef! She's okay. She's on her way home now."

"Did she say why she didn't text you back earlier?"

"No. She did say that's she's exchanged texts with her mother, though." I sighed. "I'm tired, Robert. How far have we walked? About eight kilometres? Ten?"

"I don't know. It's not far now, Chloe."

Twenty minutes later, we reached our street. It was a mess. Liquifaction covered one side of it for fifty metres or so, but we managed to get past without wrecking our shoes even more than they had already been wrecked, though that would probably have been impossible. I just wanted to be home, to sit in our living room with a hot green tea, then go and lie on my bed and read quietly, and put this horrible day behind me.

But it wasn't going to work out like that. We reached our house—the new house that we'd only been in for a couple of weeks—and stood on the footpath, astounded. One side of the roof had collapsed inwards, leaving a gaping hole about the size of a small car over my bedroom. A piece of paper, probably a sheet of the notes I'd made from yesterday's lectures, silently drifted out and floated away in the breeze, disappearing over our neighbour's fence. The chimney had toppled, partly onto the garden path below, and partly inwards into my room.

I think I screamed then. I don't remember. I do remember crying, falling to the ground, even lying on the ground. Maybe I banged my fists on the hard turf too. But only for a minute or so. Then I composed myself and looked up. I watched Robert as he strolled around the perimeter of the house, staring up at the damage, until he passed out of sight. For a moment, I felt hurt that he hadn't made an effort to comfort me, but I know he wouldn't even have thought of that. It didn't matter though.

Suddenly, I thought Robert might not be safe.

"Robert! Move away from the house! What if there's another earthquake?"

He emerged from around the corner of the house,

glanced at me and stepped a metre or so further back, then walked around the back of the house. Probably to check on possible damage there.

"Chloe!"

I turned and saw Stef coming up the driveway, and gasped in both relief and shock. Before I could say anything, she reached me and grabbed me in a fierce hug. Normally, I would push someone away if she did that, but not Stef. I just disengaged myself from her embrace and stepped back. I knew not to ask if she was okay. No one in this city would be okay. In fact, that's the most common lie Non-Spectrum people use, saying they're 'fine' or 'okay' when they're not, so there's no point asking, really.

"Are you hurt?" I asked. "You look awful."

Stef stared at me with wide eyes. Her mouth drooped open almost inhumanly, like in Edward Munch's *The Scream*, but she remained silent. She raked her fingers down her face. Her fingernails were filthy, like she had been weeding in the garden without gloves.

Something was wrong. I was sure of it. More than what had happened to Robert and me, the flaking of the ceiling in the library, the raining down of the plaster ceiling tiles in the lecture theatre, the traipsing home ten kilometres through the worst traffic I'd ever seen to discover our wrecked house.

Stef lurched at me again, wrapping me up in her arms. This time I stayed where I was because she started sobbing on my shoulder and I couldn't pull away. Instead, I gave her a hug. At least, I tried to. She probably expected it. I put my arms around her and squeezed her a bit. I patted her on the back like I've seen people do on TV. But I didn't go as far as saying, "It's okay, you'll be fine," because I didn't think she would be.

After a minute or so of this, I got uncomfortable and pushed her away gently. "Tell me what happened."

Stef wiped her eyes with a soggy handkerchief. "We all left the office after the quake to gather outside until it was safe. Then someone called out and said that the CTV building had collapsed. That's just down the road. Some of us ran down there to see if we could do anything." She paused to wipe her eyes again. "There was just one wall left standing, and part of it was on fire. A few people got out. I heard someone say she was on the top floor when the earthquake struck, then the building went down, and she stepped out at ground level. Most of the survivors were from the top floor."

I felt chilled at this. "What about everyone else?" I asked, though I didn't need to hear the answer.

Stef made a little squeaking sound, as if she was trying not to cry again. "We dug with our hands where we could reach, trying to find survivors. Then the fire service and the demolition crews came with their machinery to help with the search. Lots of people must have died in there."

"How terrible," said Robert. I hadn't noticed him coming to join us as I was so focused on what Stef was saying. He must have finished his examination of the house.

"The proper rescue crews sent us away after a while. Someone from the office gave me a lift home. I can't get my own car. It's stuck in Lichfield Street car park. That's been closed and no one's allowed in."

I couldn't think of anything to say, so I stayed quiet.

"I see our house is munted too," continued Stef, glancing up at the damage.

"Munted?" said Robert. "What does that mean?"

"Wrecked. Destroyed." Stef shook her head. I didn't

know why. Maybe she didn't want to discuss it any more right now.

"I looked through the windows," said Robert. "It's wrecked, all right. The kitchen is a mess of broken glass and plates and spilled food. The cupboard doors have all swung open, and it looks like most of the food and crockery got shaken out. The fridge has fallen over too, and it's blocking the door, so we probably won't be able to get in that way."

"We're not going in there!" I said. "It'll be too fucking dangerous, Robert! Are you out of your mind?"

"I thought we might want to get some of our stuff," he muttered.

"No bloody way!"

"The living room is worse, though."

"How can it be worse?"

"The TV's fallen over and smashed. The bookcase too. The wooden floor's all warped, and it looks like there's a large molehill in one corner that's spread liquifaction sludge all over the floor. I couldn't see into any other rooms."

"Shit!" I couldn't think of much to say except expletives. At least I could think of plenty of those.

"Oh, and it looks like the staircase has become detached from the top floor and is hanging at a strange angle, so even if we get inside, we wouldn't be able to go up to our rooms to get anything."

"Bloody hell," said Stef. "All our clothes and stuff are in there."

"They'll have to stay there. It's too dangerous to go in," I repeated.

"It'll be red-stickered, obviously," said Robert. "Has anyone seen Sex?"

"No," I said, horrified. I hadn't even given a thought to

our little cat until now. "Do you think she's... dead?"

"I hope not," said Robert, "but she might be trapped inside, and we can't get in there to look for her."

"Don't worry, you two," said Stef. "She's probably all right. Cats seem to know when an earthquake's about to happen. She would have gone to hide somewhere until it's all over."

"But it is all over now."

"Well, she'll come back soon, I'm sure. We can look for her later. We have to work out what we're going to do. Obviously, we can't stay here."

"So, where shall we go?" asked Robert. "My mum's? Though I don't know how we would get there. It's too far to walk." He grimaced. Perhaps he'd already changed his mind about whether that was a good choice anyway.

"Marinda's, maybe," said Stef, "though I still haven't heard from her. I tried calling her after I texted you, but she didn't answer. I left a message."

"Her new house is near here, isn't it?" I asked. Marinda had bought a house while I was overseas, her first step on the property ladder.

"It's in Linwood. Tancred Street. We can walk there easily enough. I hope she has power and water and her house is okay. I wish she'd hurry up and call me back, but, as you probably know, she's not very reliable."

"Did we have a survival pack ready?" I asked. "You know, water, radio, candles, food, spare clothes..."

"It's in the house," groaned Stef. "We can't get to it."

"Let's walk to Marinda's house, then," I said. "Maybe her phone needs charging and that's why she hasn't replied."

"Okay. I can let us in. She keeps a spare key under a

loose paving stone in the garden. I'm sure she won't mind. I hope she has running water. I'm filthy."

Though it was only a couple of kilometres walk, it took us over an hour, during which further aftershocks shook us physically and mentally. Debris and road closures forced us to take several diversions. On one corner, an old shop had collapsed into a ragged pile of bricks and wood. Emergency services were outside. Other buildings had also fallen or looked broken beyond repair. Potholes and even larger sinkholes spotted the roads and footpaths. We saw a car, nose-down, half-buried in one, abandoned by the driver. Above all of this, there was a constant buzzing of military helicopters flying to and from the central city.

My nerves jangled like loose bracelets on someone playing the maracas. We reached Marinda's house and, mercifully, it appeared intact and undamaged. But would it have water and power? I wondered.

"Her car's not here," said Stef, "but I'll knock, just in case she walked home."

She knocked. I stood on the doorstep behind her, waiting impatiently. I was hungry and thirsty now, and truly upset by the events of the day. Robert wandered around the garden, looking all over the house, probably for signs of damage.

There was no response to Stef's knocking so, after a minute or two, she lifted the loose paving stone in the back garden, retrieved the secret key and let us into the house.

Robert flipped the light switch in the kitchen. The light didn't come on. I groaned in disappointment. Hopefully, we would have more luck with the water. I turned on the tap over the kitchen sink. Nothing came out.

"There's no water either," I called out.

"If there was," said Stef, "we would have to boil it first.

It might be contaminated. But there's no power to boil it anyway."

I remembered that we'd had to do that after the September earthquake. Broken sewage pipes had rendered the water unsafe to drink until they had been repaired. Today was probably a repeat of that. *Déjà poo*. Same old crap.

Robert came back into the kitchen. He'd apparently been through the house, checking for damage. "Lots of things have fallen from the shelves in the living room and from a bookcase in the hallway. I'll tidy those up. That'll save Marinda a job when she gets home."

"I'll see if I can make us a sandwich or something," said Stef, opening the fridge. "This food is going to spoil soon anyway. We may as well use it before it does."

"I'll look for bottled water," I said. Marinda would probably have some. Since the last big earthquake in September, everyone keeps a large supply of it.

A few minutes later, we were eating tuna and cheese sandwiches on wholemeal bread in the living room, listening to the coverage of the earthquake and the unfolding recovery operations on a battery-powered radio that I found in one of the kitchen cupboards.

"I can't believe this has happened to our city," said Stef. I didn't reply. I just kept listening to the broadcast, numbed by the relentless stream of grim news. Most of the CBD cordoned off. Extensive damage. More people found dead. Perpetual aftershocks. Most of the city expected to be without power and water for days; some of the eastern suburbs not expected to get power or water for weeks.

This was getting too much for me.

"I can't listen to this anymore," said Robert, echoing my own thoughts. "I'm going to dig a hole in the back garden that we can use as a toilet." He went out to look in the shed for a spade.

"Let's switch it off, Stef."

"Okay. For a while." She switched off the radio and picked up her cell phone. "I'm going to call Marinda again."

I watched her intently as she dialled, listened and then closed her phone.

"It went to voicemail again. She still isn't answering. I'm worried about her, Chloe."

I didn't know what to say, but I was worried too.

CHAPTER FOUR

I'm finally sleeping, and it's the same day all over again. I don't know how I know this; in my dream, I just do. I'm not at uni this time, I'm somewhere in town; High Street, I think. It's lunchtime, with crowds of people scurrying about doing errands in their lunch hour or buying food. I walk amongst them, but they don't look at me like people usually do. No, I'm not walking at all... I float between them, and I don't think they can see me.

Now I hover above them, looking down. People pass beneath me, oblivious to me and to what is about to happen. It's a beautiful, warm day. I look around. There are many old buildings here, some of which surely won't survive the earthquake. I can't imagine it as it is now, hours later, in real life, because I won't see this part of town afterwards. It's deep inside the Red Zone cordon.

I realise that some of the people in my dream may be about to be injured or killed. I know the earthquake is coming soon; my dream-mind informs me so. I try speaking to someone, but he walks past. I don't think he can hear me or see me. I feel helpless that I can't connect with them.

Then I see Marinda. She's on the footpath on the other side of the road, looking in a shop window. I float across the road towards her. I'm just above her now, and I reach down to grab her shoulder, but she moves away. I know that I must warn her urgently. I call her name, but she doesn't react. I float after her, but it's too late. Below me, the ground ripples like loose corrugated iron roofing in a gale. I see Marinda drop, or perhaps stumble, to the ground in front of an old shop. The front wall of the shop comes away and topples towards her. I scream silently and reach out with arms of mist as if I can somehow prevent it from falling, but I cannot.

Now it is later, sometime in the future, maybe days or weeks away, and it is night time. I am in another part of the CBD, though obviously still inside the Red Zone. Around me are piles of rubble, some shops in ruins, and some intact but probably unsafe to enter. It is dark and deadly quiet. There is no sign of anyone. I wonder why I am here.

I'm on the ground, and I walk down the centre of the road. I don't recognise which road it is because it's too dark and most of the buildings I might have recognised lie in broken pieces. I sense that my walk takes me towards the cathedral, which everyone used to be able to see at night because it was lit up for the tourists. The cathedral spire is no longer there; it lies in front of the ruined cathedral like a soldier fallen from the battlements. There is nothing to light up. The sky is dark, apart from one bright beam of light that moves in circles—the searchlight of hope, reflecting off the scattered clouds.

I turn a corner into another road. There are some newer buildings here amongst the old ones, and they appear undamaged. I recognise a café that I've eaten at a few times with Stef. It's upstairs, above a clothing shop, and before I can wonder how to get up there, I find myself sitting at one of the tables. There's an unfinished coffee and a piece of stale cake sitting there, covered in dust and mould, part of someone's lunch that will never be finished.

After a few moments, I realise that I am not alone.

With the aid of starlight through the windows, I can make out the shape of another person sitting at a nearby table. No, there are two of them. I'm apprehensive, but also curious, and I go over to them.

"What are you doing here?" I say.

One of them turns towards me. He must have heard me. I gasp in shock when I see his bruised, bloodied and gashed face. His arm is bent at an impossible angle.

"We're waiting until it is safe," he says. His misshapen mouth makes his words indistinct. I barely understand them.

"Our family will be all right," said the other, a woman, in a strange voice. "We'll wait here for them. Until the earthquake's over."

I look at her with horror. Her wispy, elongated and inhuman face stares back at me. Her appearance is wraith-like. Fog-like arms curl above her head, and everything below her waist is nebulous and shadowy.

"The earthquake was over a long time ago," I whisper.

"Can't you feel it?" said the man. "I nearly shit myself when it started."

"We're going to wait here for our coffee. We ordered coffee, and we're going to wait here," said the woman. Her voice is now a snarl, her face tinged with red.

I back away from them, afraid now. I want to get away from this place, but I don't know how. I don't know how I even got here, or why I was here. I feel dreadful, stuck in a nightmare that is out of control in my mind.

Then I wake up, sweating and feeling sick.

I get out of bed, go into Robert's room, and climb into bed with him. I don't wake him. I just want him near.

A few shops and supermarkets opened the day after the earthquake, following a clean-up. The quake had destroyed several, though, so the few that were open were busy. The shelves that normally held bottled water were empty. Robert came back from early-morning foraging with some milk and some diet coke.

Stef had tried several more times to reach Marinda, but her calls always went to voicemail. Mid-morning, Stef called the police to file a missing persons report and discovered that Ingrid had already done that as the next of kin. We decided we would stay in Marinda's house and look after it for her until we knew what had happened to her. Perhaps she had lost her phone and gone to stay at a friend's house but, by now, we feared the worst.

We still had a small supply of Marinda's bottled water for drinking, but there was not enough for washing or cleaning. Then Stef heard on the radio, the little battery-powered one, that water tankers had been brought in from all over New Zealand. She listened to find out the location of the nearest one, found a wheeled suitcase from amongst Marinda's things, put the water bottles that we'd emptied into it and wheeled it to the tanker, which was almost two kilometres distant. Meanwhile, Robert started to tidy up the house, replacing all the items that had fallen off shelves and out of cupboards, apart from those which were broken and could only be thrown away.

My laptop was almost out of battery, and I realised that I actually did not want to do without it, so I searched for an alternate power source. I discovered that Marinda's house had two flat plate solar panels on the roof that partially heated the stored water in the hot cylinder tank. That stored water would allow us to wash for a day or two, but we wouldn't be able to drink it. Seeing as we had no water supply anyway, I decided to divert the solar power for my own needs somehow. The 'somehow' was the tricky bit.

I poked around in Marinda's cluttered garage for a while and came across a 200Ah solar battery, still in its original packaging. Marinda must have bought it to use with the solar panels, but either didn't know how to connect it or hadn't got around to it. I couldn't believe my luck when I found a set of cables with it and a DC/AC inverter. I now had all I required, so I just needed to put it all together.

There was an old, paint-splotched metal ladder in the garage. I dragged it out and leaned it up against the house. A minute and a half later, I was lying prone on the roof, examining the solar panels, when Robert called out to me from below.

"Chloe! What the hell are you doing up there?"

I turned around and poked my head over the edge of the roof. "I'm trying to see how to reroute the solar power for my laptop," I called. "I saw something about this in a science magazine about a year ago. I'm sure I can do it. Give me a few minutes."

"Be careful! If there's another earthquake, you might get shaken off the roof!"

He was right about that, of course, so I hurried. I knew what I had to do, and I soon worked out it was not anything on the roof. I had to get into the attic instead. I shimmied down the ladder and hunted around inside the house for an access point into the attic. When I found it, I got the ladder and dragged it inside. Climbing up with a torch, I pushed aside the lid covering the access point, poked my head into the attic space and shone the torch around in a slow arc.

I groaned. A complex, symmetrical structure of wooden rafters criss-crossed the entire space. I pulled myself up and carefully clambered through them, taking care to step on the wooden beams so that I did not put my foot through the ceiling. Though I suppose it wouldn't matter so much if I did. Gradually, I clambered through the rafters to where the cable from the solar panels on the roof came in.

After I reached that point, I lay supported on the network of wooden beams, contemplating the next step. Somehow, I had to disconnect that cable from the water heating system and reconnect it to the solar battery I'd found, which I'd left downstairs in Marinda's room on her dressing table. I had a picture in my mind of the illustrations I'd seen in the science magazine article a year ago, and I hoped they were accurate or, if they weren't accurate, that I wouldn't set the house alight or cause something equally disastrous.

"Chloe! Chloe!" The sound of Robert shouting my name from the floor below broke the flow of my thoughts. I spun around slowly so I didn't hit my head on the wooden beams criss-crossing all around me.

"What?" I snapped back at him, annoyed that he'd interrupted me. He didn't appear to notice my irritation.

"You didn't hear me when I called you at first. I've made a fire in a hole in the back garden, and I'm boiling some water in a saucepan. Do you want a hot drink?"

"Yes," I said. Of course I did. He didn't need to ask me, did he?

"Okay. I don't know how long it will take. I'll call you. I'm going back out to dig a hole for another toilet now."

At this rate, there won't be much left of the garden soon. I forced my concentration back onto recollecting the contents of the solar powered laptop article that I'd read long ago. Three minutes later, I'd figured it out. I half-crawled, half-climbed through the network of rafters, pulling the cable with me, until I was above Marinda's room. Balancing myself on one of the solid beams, I reached through the soft, fluffy pink insulation, unscrewed a downlight fitting from a small recess in the ceiling and peered through to confirm that I actually was above her room and not the toilet next to it.

I didn't replace the light fitting. There was no point anyway as we had no power, but I did inspect it, as the shape and vital statistics of light bulbs are fascinating to me. It was a common type, so I quickly lost interest in it.

Then I threaded the cable through the recess into the room as far as it would go, which I unfortunately discovered was not even far enough to reach the floor.

"Shit." I hadn't anticipated this. I noticed for the first time that I was sweating from all the effort and from the heat trapped in the attic. Sweaty grime and dust covered my face, hair and bare arms. I lifted my sleeveless top (my usual Tuesday black one, even though it was Wednesday, because I did not have any other clothes anymore) and wiped my forehead and nose.

"The drinks are ready!" called out Robert from below.

I could certainly use a drink now, even a hot one. In eagerness, I stood up too abruptly in the confined space and bumped the side of my head against a rafter. That threw me off balance, and I stumbled backwards. I jammed my right foot down to prevent myself from falling. This move failed because my foot did not land on a solid wooden beam, but on the soft, fluffy pink insulation. With a cracking sound, my foot plunged through the ceiling, and before I could fall and cause even more damage or hurt myself, I grabbed a rafter with my left hand and steadied myself.

I pulled my foot out, dislodging bits of plaster that fell to the floor below. I swivelled around, leaned over the hole

I'd just made in the ceiling and looked down at Marinda's bed in the room below.

"I'm okay!" I called out. "I'm not hurt!"

"Good!" shouted Robert. He'd already left the room.

I went down the ladder and, after quaffing the green tea Robert had made for me, I returned to Marinda's room. The cable from the solar panels dangled well above floor level, but I could still make it work. I put the 200Ah solar battery on top of the bookcase and connected the cable to it. Then I fetched the DC/AC converter from the garage and connected it to the solar battery with an extension lead. Finally, I was able to connect this to my laptop, which I put on the bed and turned on with keen anticipation.

It worked. When my laptop came on, it started charging from the solar panels. The solar battery would collect enough excess energy to keep it running all day and night.

I wiped my sticky, sweaty forehead with my sleeveless top again, nodded slightly to myself with satisfaction and went outside so I could share my success with Robert. Stef had returned with a suitcase-full of bottled water, and Robert was helping her unload them.

"Robert! I've got it working! I've got the laptop working off the solar panels." I said.

"That's great, Chloe!" he replied.

Stef just stared in my direction. Maybe she didn't know what to say, or maybe she didn't appreciate the genius of what I'd achieved. Or perhaps she was upset because Robert had told her that I'd put my foot through the ceiling in Marinda's room. I didn't know. But I guess I was about to find out.

"I'm going to look for Sex," said Robert, and he walked

off.

Once the adrenalin of the day of the earthquake had passed, and the realisation of how much life had changed sunk in, I felt emotionally drained. I became quieter and withdrew from Robert and Stef. Five days passed like this in an uncomfortable blur. Some of the city returned to a kind of normal. Unfortunately, we were still without both power and water after this time, though those services had been restored to the western suburbs by now. But we were better off than suburbs further to the east. Some of those would never again be habitable because of the ground damage. And in the centre of town, the army had set up patrolled blockades on every road, creating a cordon around the area so that no one could enter while the search and recovery continued, and the demolitions began.

We hadn't been able to find our cat. Robert had been back to our old house twice a day to look for her, calling her name, but to no avail. We'd almost given up hope of ever finding her again. I was sad about not knowing what had happened to her.

Robert seemed concerned about me, for I spent most of my time lying on the floor in Marinda's room, though I was actually using it as my room, staring at my laptop, checking the latest quake information on GeoNet and reading the online news reports. I don't even know why I did that, but it did seem that I was fixated on this. In truth, I didn't feel like doing anything else at all. I'd become obsessed with checking the latest quake data, day and night. I'd wake up with any aftershock above a 'three' in the hills, or a 'three point something' elsewhere, then get up to check GeoNet and wait for it to display the details about where the epicentre was and what magnitude and depth it was. Sometimes, I had only two or three hours sleep in a night; other nights, four or five. It was as if Mother Earth determined how little I would sleep. And everyone else in Christchurch, probably.

I knew that I was traumatised by the earthquake and the ongoing aftershocks, and deeply upset by Marinda's disappearance, but it was much more than that. I had never spent as much time with Marinda as I had done with Stef. Maybe it was because she was ten years older, or maybe because she was doing well in her career and had no behavioural or neurological differences, and I felt that I didn't fit into her world. But she was missing, her body probably lying undiscovered under some rubble in the Red Zone, just like in my dream. Though Stef hadn't given up hope that she would appear as if out of nowhere, alive and well, I already thought of her as dead.

It all seemed so abrupt, so finite, so permanent. I'd never even got the chance to say goodbye in person, yet I was now living in her house, wearing her clothes (as, like Stef, I only had the ones I was wearing that fateful day, and Marinda was the same size as me), eating her tinned food and sleeping in her bed. We would probably have been driving her car if we knew where it was, but maybe it was trapped in a car park building like The Frog, Stef's car. It seemed to me that I was trying to take over Marinda's identity or something, or merge hers with mine, stealthily but unintentionally, and maybe losing some of my own identity in the process. I no longer had any possessions, apart from my laptop and the clothes I was wearing on the day of the earthquake, and Marinda's things were all undamaged, but she was missing, probably dead. I kind of felt that I was not letting her rest in peace because I was quite literally wearing her shoes.

My mind was numb. It had pretty much just shut down. I'm sure there were things I should have been thinking of, people I should contact, places I had to be, but that part of my mind just didn't work now. The abruptness of the earthquake and the sudden change in every routine part of my life had rendered me temporarily incapable of doing any of those things. Instead, I tried to control these feelings and thoughts by immersing myself in the raw data, the graphs and charts of the aftershocks, the news reports and eyewitness accounts, the missing persons list, the maps of the cordoned-off areas, the lists of the to-be-demolished buildings and anything else I could find. In some part of my mind, I thought that if I could understand and quantify everything that had happened, it would make it easier to cope with somehow. But this process was stressful in itself. I had trouble reading the aftershock magnitudes and depths because of my dyscalculia, though I could make sense of the bar charts.

At least with the delivery of port-a-loos in the street, we didn't have to shit and pee in a bucket or a hole in the ground anymore. That was a slight improvement, but it wasn't pleasant to have to walk fifty metres down the street if we needed the port-a-loo at night, so we used the bucket then. For showers, we walked down to the portable shower trailer set up in a local car park. It was cold and barely private.

Apart from these ablutions and my obsessive earthquake data watching, I did extremely little. Stef went back to work after three days. Her office relocated itself from the CBD to Phillipstown, which, fortunately for her, was walking distance from Marinda's house. She was peeved at not having her car though, as it was still trapped in the car park building, and we didn't know when it would be deemed safe to retrieve it. She left early in the morning each weekday, so I rarely saw her then.

Robert kept himself busy. He stayed out of the house a

lot because there was no power or water. He went early to university when it reopened, and came home late. When he wasn't there, he worked as a volunteer for the Student Army, clearing liquifaction from city streets and people's properties. I think he spent some time at his mum's too. Keeping really full-on occupied all the time was his way of coping with the disaster, I realised.

So he didn't have much time for me. I made it difficult for him, anyway. I wouldn't get up in the morning until I had reviewed any overnight data that I'd missed, so he ate his breakfast alone before going out. I seldom descended the stairs to eat dinner either. I usually asked Stef to bring something up to my room so I could continue using my laptop. Nor did I feel like inviting Robert to my bed. When he came to talk to me, even just to ask how I was feeling, I was either too engrossed to respond and ignored him until he left, or I swore and shouted at him to leave me alone. I vaguely realised I was pushing him away, but I couldn't even tear myself away from my self-imposed compulsive task to talk about it, let alone do anything about it.

I felt so tired. All I wanted was to be alone, and do nothing in my aloneness except think about what had befallen us and immerse myself in information about it, as if I could somehow understand it that way. My thoughts became increasingly gloomy, despondent and depressing with each passing day. I was aware of it, but for some reason I couldn't grasp, I just didn't care anymore. I was *exhaustipated*. Too tired to give a crap.

This went on for a few days before Stef and Robert must have decided to confront me about it. Again, I hadn't gone down to breakfast. I was lying on the bed with my laptop for once, instead of on the floor, when they both came into my room early one morning and sat on the bed on either side of me. I had the impression that they were surrounding me so I couldn't avoid them any longer. A jolt of claustrophobia shot through my body like the shiver of someone in Norway skinny-dipping in an icy pond.

"Are you going to university today, Chloe?" asked Robert. He glanced at me when he'd finished saying this, as if prompting me to answer. That's one of the mannerisms I'd mentored him in.

"I don't think so," I sighed without taking my eyes off the screen. "What day is it anyway?"

"Monday," said Stef. "And I have to go to work in a few minutes. But Robert and I, well, we're worried about you, Chloe. We understand that what you're doing is a coping strategy, but it's not good for you, not after all this time. And you're not getting much sleep either, are you?"

"Yeah," I said, surprising myself. It is seldom that I'm ever so terse.

"We know the earthquake and Marinda's disappearance really upset you," said Robert. I noticed he said 'disappearance' rather than death.

"Me too," said Stef, wiping at an eye. "I miss Marinda so much, but there's nothing I can do about that, until we hear from her or from the authorities. Life goes on, as the saying goes. It's important to get back on the horse."

"What horse?" I glanced at Robert. He shrugged. Clearly, he didn't know what Stef meant either.

"A metaphorical horse, of course. What I mean is: you just have to get back to normal, to doing the usual things. If you don't go back to uni soon, you'll never catch up. You don't want to drop out a second time, do you?"

I felt like shaking my head 'no', but I didn't do it. I just sat quietly, expressionlessly, contemplating it. I'd dropped out in my first year at uni, two years ago, because I was a complete emotional mess. That was before I started on a series of juggling psychotic medications to find out what worked and what didn't. Then a thought struck me, and I sat bolt upright, startling them both.

"Shit!"

"What?" said Stef and Robert together.

"My meds!"

"What about them?" asked Robert.

"You have been taking them, haven't you?" asked Stef.

"Oh, the earthquake... were they all inside the house?"

"Yes," I said. "All of them, and they're all gone now. I completely forgot about them. I mean, I didn't forget at first, I just was too much in shock to care. And then too engrossed in this earthquake data study to remember. So I haven't had any since the earthquake!"

"I wondered why I didn't see any in the bathroom cabinet," said Robert, "but I thought you might be keeping them with you. You should always have a supply in your bag anyway, just in case."

"Just in case of what? Our house is destroyed? You know, I never thought of that," I mocked.

"Is that why you've been feeling low and behaving a bit strangely?" asked Stef. "Because you haven't been taking your meds? I thought it was post-quake stress."

"I don't know." I sighed. "Both, probably."

"Shit." Robert echoed the thoughts in my head. He knew how dangerous a situation it could be to alter meds abruptly. "You'd better see your doctor as soon as possible, Chloe. Urgently. It's really important. You taught me that."

"I know that." Maybe I snarled at him a little. He shrank away from me.

"I'm just trying to help."

"I know. Sorry."

"Look, I've got to go," said Stef, getting to her feet. "Are you going to be okay, Chloe?"

"Sure," I said. Actually, I probably wouldn't be, but I just couldn't face the consequences of saying that. Saying I'd be okay is the expected response anyway.

"Why don't you get up and come to uni with me today, Chloe?" said Robert as Stef left the room with a smile and a goodbye wave.

"But—is it safe at the university? Are lectures continuing?"

"Yes, they are. The library's closed, but they've set up giant marquee tents in the grounds, and lectures are being conducted in those."

"Wow. I didn't know that."

"So, come with me. Get back into your normal study routine. I'm sure you'll feel much better if you do. But make sure you call your doctor today. That's really important, Chloe."

"I know. Stop mothering me." I was finding his attention annoying now. Robert seldom gave up on a point he wanted to make until he had made it far beyond the point it needed to be made.

"I'm going to catch the bus in half an hour, so be ready then if you decide to come with me." He stood and went out. I watched him as he headed back to his own room. For a few moments, I wondered if the stress of the earthquake had strained our relationship too much. We hadn't spent much time together lately, not like we used to do. Had it fallen apart without me even noticing?

I'll have to talk to Robert about that, I thought. First, the doctor. No, wait, the doctors' surgery won't be open yet. I'll call later.

I stood. Just having this short conversation with Robert and Stef had been helpful. I felt it breaking me free of the OCD pattern. Maybe just a little, but that was a start. Robert was probably right. If I went back to uni and tried to do all my usual things, maybe I wouldn't feel so compelled to follow the quake statistics and charts all the time. Maybe I would feel a lot better, and soon.

I glanced around me. A pile of unwashed clothes lay on the floor by the window, as I hadn't done any washing for days. That, at least, was not uncommon, though, at the moment, it was because we still didn't have any water. The remains of last night's fish and chips sat wrapped up, unloved and abandoned, on the desk. I decided to put them out of the window for the birds to eat.

I sighed. I'd barely had the energy or willpower to go out anywhere, like to a café or someplace, since the earthquake. That was highly unusual. Unprecedented, even. But I sensed that was changing.

CHAPTER FIVE

I might be about to lose my label, and I'm not sure exactly how I feel about that. It's part of me now; I accept it unreservedly, and it defines who am I and to what community I belong. I have Asperger's Syndrome. Those of us with this diagnosis call ourselves Aspies. That's who we are.

But the American Psychiatric Association, in their collective wisdom, may be about to change all of that with the new edition of their iconic bestseller, the Diagnostic and Statistical Manual of Mental Disorders (the DSM-V), the first for nearly twenty years. In it, they intend to remove the category of Asperger's Syndrome altogether, and along with PDD-NOS, merge it into the overall category of ASD (Autistic Spectrum Disorder).

Though it took me some time to digest and understand the implications of my Asperger's Syndrome diagnosis, I feel that if this label is removed, it will be like tearing away part of my identity. The part that I have in common with people who have the same way of thinking and feeling as me. The way of being that separates us from everyone else in the world, those with Neuro-Typical Syndrome, I call them. I've got attached to my label. I don't want to lose it.

So, instead of being Aspies, we could call ourselves WASPies... Were Asperger's Syndrome People. But even that would take some mental adjustment to get used to.

Why is this change being made anyway? Was the Asperger's community consulted at all? I wasn't asked about it.

Nothing about us, without us. Please.

I packed up my bag and went to uni with Robert. He was right; getting back to so-called normal did make me feel better, though the lectures were in marquees and I couldn't go into the library. We even had hot drinks in one of our favourite cafés, as we had done for almost all of the previous year.

Between lectures, I powered up my laptop. I made a conscious effort not to check the quake statistics whenever an aftershock occurred, for if I did, I would soon get pulled back into the same depressing, OCD behaviour. I checked my emails instead, and found there were dozens. I went through them as rapidly as possible, almost like an automaton on speed, mostly deleting, but cursorily replying to a few. To give myself a boost of energy, after a green tea I tried espressos and triple-shot lattes. They tasted so good, I wondered why I hadn't tried them before. By the third one of those I was buzzing, and I loved the feeling. For the first time since my return from Australia, I felt happy and energetic.

At 11.14 a.m., I remembered to call the doctor's surgery. Once I'd finished my latte, I flipped open my mobile phone.

"Hello, can I have an appointment with Doctor Penny, please?"

"I'm sorry, but Penny is away this week. Would you like to see someone else?"

"Um... no, thanks, I'll wait." I wasn't comfortable seeing a doctor I didn't know. Surely, I could wait a few more days. I was certainly feeling much better. Getting up and about and away from the house was all the panacea I needed, perhaps. I hung up.

I went for a walk around the campus, thinking about whether delaying seeing a doctor was a good idea or not. I wasn't supposed to come off my meds abruptly like I had done. I'd thought about it a few weeks before, and decided to wait for a 'sign' to indicate to me when I should try cutting them back, but abandoning them altogether was completely different. Not that it was my fault. But there had certainly been a sign, I guess. All my meds rendered unreachable by the earthquake.

Had they been helping, or not? I did seem okay now, so maybe it would be all right if I didn't take them anymore. Besides, with Doctor Penny away, if I saw someone else, he or she would have to pull my current medical file out of a filing cabinet (actually, I believe I had an entire filing cabinet all to myself) and ask me lots of awkward questions that I wouldn't feel like answering to someone I don't know.

I decided I would stay off the meds until Penny gets back, at least, as an experiment. After all, I'd got through moving house abruptly (twice), the earthquake, the disappearance and probable death of my cousin and the loss of my cat, which was altogether a tremendous amount of change, and I think I'd coped with it all right, or at least much better than it might otherwise have been, so I should be able to cope without my pills for a few more days. Maybe I just didn't need them anymore.

The other thing was that now I was not obsessing about the quake statistics, I'd realised I was feeling much better than I'd felt for ages, even despite the earthquake. Perhaps that had been a kind of catalyst for me to re-evaluate my life's priorities or something. Or maybe to be thankful for the things I had, which consisted of my savings, my laptop and a few threadbare second-hand clothes. Obviously, there were a lot fewer things now because so many of them had been lost in the house destroyed by the earthquake, including all of my clothes and my entire book collection. I'd kind of had a minimalist lifestyle forced upon me, but I didn't mind. I felt as if I'd cut loose the shackles of materiality holding me back, and now I felt uplifted; soaring, even. It felt like a new beginning for me. It was a glorious feeling, and it imbued me with heaps more energy than I usually had. Perhaps that's why I hadn't been sleeping much.

My phone rang, and I answered it.

"Hello?"

"Ms Wilson?"

"Yes. Who's this?"

"I'm calling from Hillmorton Hospital about your mother. She's been rather unsettled since the earthquake, upset and anxious. According to our records, you haven't visited her for a while, and I thought—well—that it might cheer her up a bit if you did. She doesn't get many visitors these days. Are you planning to visit any time soon?"

"No," I said. Guiltily, I realised I hadn't even thought about it during my bout of OCD and depressive behaviour.

"Oh! Well, do you have a message that I can pass on to her?"

"I'll come to visit her soon."

"Oh! I thought you just said you weren't planning to come in soon."

"No, I said that I *hadn't* planned to come in. But I will. Soon."

"Well, that's good. I'll let her know. I'm sure she'll be pleased to hear that. She's been asking after you."

"Thanks for letting me know."

I rang off. I didn't actually want to go to visit my mother, but felt I should out of duty. We didn't like each other much. Nor did my father like her or me. It's a total myth that families are always full of love for each other. Sometimes, they're not. In our case, we were all better without each other. However, I would visit my mother because she'd asked. Soon. Once I'd psychologically prepared myself for the encounter.

After lunch, I went to my afternoon lecture, but I couldn't concentrate on the topic at all. I sat at the back. The professor looked like a tiny ant scuttling around, talking and showing a sequence of Powerpoint slides that I couldn't see clearly. I didn't hear what he was saying because my earphones were in and I was listening to *Adele* while browsing Facebook on my laptop. It was hard to keep still, and I squirmed on my seat, jiggled my legs restlessly and tapped my feet to the rhythm of the music. A neighbouring student reached over, prodded me on the knee and mouthed something to me that I couldn't understand because I can't lip-read. I scowled at her and pushed her hand away roughly. Maybe I'd irritated her with my movements, but I didn't care.

Later that afternoon, I sat in the café having another triple-shot latte and horizontally spinning my pen in my left hand while I worked through my Psych reading. The textbook wasn't taxing; instead, I understood it all instantly as if some futuristic *Star Trek* device had plugged the information directly into my brain. This is great, I thought. My mind's so sharp, so clear now. It must be because I've stopped taking those damned meds.

A loud burst of laughter from a group of people at a neighbouring table interrupted my thoughts. Normally, I would say nothing about it and, if they continued annoying me, I would simply leave, but not this time. I spun my pen one last time, caught it between thumb and forefinger, and spoke even before I thought about it.

"Will you shut up over there? I'm trying to read here. You're disturbing me!"

A young guy in a blue felt hat and blue sweatshirt swivelled in his chair to face me. "Are you talking to us?" he said, his mouth oddly askew.

"Yeah, I'm talking to you, shit-for-brains. I'm reading here. Be quieter."

"Look, I don't know who you think you are, but you can't talk to me like that. This isn't the library. We'll talk if we want to."

"No, you can shut the fuck up. I'm trying to read!" I said all this without thinking. Actually, it seemed to me that I was listening to myself talk, or rather, listening to someone else talk with my voice. I'm usually not this rude and disrespectful so quickly. Normally, it takes a few minutes.

Blue Hat's nose flared, and his eyes blazed with a *bitch-stare*. After a few moments, his face relaxed, and he said, "You've got some serious issues, dude. Go to the library if you want to read." He turned away.

I seethed as he and his friends laughed again, their raucous outburst rattling my brain like a picket fence in an earthquake. I looked around and saw several other students staring at me, having suspended their own quiet conversations to see and hear what was going on in my corner of the café. I scowled at them, and most of them looked away.

"Are you all right, Chloe?" Robert sat down next to me.

"You sound angry."

"I'm pissed off at the noise in here!" I said, raising my voice for the last four words. Blue Hat and his friends ignored me.

"I can see that," said Robert, and I realised that I must appear terribly upset, for Robert is probably the least perspicacious person I know. He has Asperger's too, and he reads body language like he reads ancient Greek, that is, like a blind mouse reads the time. Not at all.

"It is the café, after all," continued Robert. "People are allowed to talk in here."

I sighed. "I know. I don't know why it bothered me so much. I guess I'm just not feeling like myself at the moment."

"Yeah, of course."

I didn't know what he meant by that, but I couldn't be bothered to ask. I felt too *grumpish*, and I'd probably just snap at him. Instead, I quickly packed up my things and left.

I think I forgot to say goodbye.

Something was wrong, but I didn't know what. Or maybe it was just that I felt different somehow. When I got home, I slammed the door behind me. I threw my bag onto one of Marinda's flowery sofas in the living room and myself onto the other one. I tried to work out what it was that I was feeling, but without success. All I achieved was stirring the muddied thoughts of my jumbled mind.

After less than a minute, I got up and went to make myself a green tea. Or a coffee. I couldn't even make a simple decision such as which drink to have. I stressed out about it while I waited for the saucepan to boil on the little gas-powered stove Stef had bought, the sound of the bubbling water echoing the heartbeat thumping in my head. Each second passed like half an hour. It drove me nuts. In a fit of pique, I switched it off, dashed out of the door and stomped down the street in search of a café where someone would make me a drink, quietly. There were a few near Marinda's house.

I found a small place and went inside. There was a middle-aged couple standing by the cake display, pointing at the delicacies, but I squeezed past them and advanced to the counter. A young dark-haired woman with tattoos on her arms looked up at me.

"A green tea and an espresso for me," I blurted out, finally having decided to have both. Some of the people sitting at nearby tables turned to stare at me. I scowled at them and turned back to the woman at the counter.

"Um, I was just serving these people," she said.

"No, that's all right," said the middle-aged man. "She can go first. We haven't made up our minds yet, anyway."

"Ooh, and a cake," I gushed. "Definitely a cake. Or three. What sort do you have? Oh, strawberry shortcake. And lemon meringue pie. Oh, what to have, what to have? And—and neenish tart too. I'll have one of each."

The woman with tattoos stared at me as if I was crazy. That's a look I've often seen, so I recognise it easily now. "Are you okay?" she asked.

"Sure. I feel great. Make the espresso a double." My legs felt restless, and I didn't want to stand still while she busied herself getting my drink and cakes, so I hopped from foot to foot, rocking my head from side to side as if I was listening to an imaginary beat. It's a new stim of mine, a kind of gentle work-out one. I saw Tattoo Woman glance at me, and I realised she was almost finished getting my food, which she had grouped onto several small plates crammed onto a plastic tray. I licked my lips at the sight of all those cakes, all for me to *excessorise* on.

I reached down to fish in my bag for my wallet. I'd pay with my plastic, of course; I never trusted myself to count out cash correctly. But, unfortunately, at that point I discovered that I didn't have my bag. In a brief moment of panic, I feared that it had been stolen from me, and I cast around me, glaring, my eyes blazing accusingly as I scanned the people nearby to see if any of them had my bag in their possession, but none did. Then I remembered that I'd rushed out of the house so fast that I'd not even brought the stupid bag with me.

"Shit." I stamped one foot on the ground.

"Something wrong?" asked Tattoo Woman, plunking the tray down on the counter in front of me.

"I've left my bag at home. Can I take this stuff to go? I'll come back and pay later."

"No, sorry. I can't do that. I have to ask you to pay first."

"But I just told you, I can't, I've left my money at home. I'll come back, I promise." A *paymeant*, I thought. I meant to pay for them, but I can't. Great word. Another one for my *fictionary*.

"I'm sorry, but it's café policy. You have to pay when you make your order."

I stared at the steaming espresso, the green tea and the cakes on the green plastic tray and heard myself grunt in frustration. It seemed so unfair. It wasn't my fault that I'd forgotten my money, and I would come back to pay later. If I remembered, which I should do. I have an excellent memory for things like that. Why couldn't Tattoo Woman see that? Then I thought that she might be angry that she'd made the espresso and served the cake slices, and they might all go to waste now. The drinks would be poured away, anyway, even if she puts the cakes back in the cabinet. But I didn't want her to do that because they were mine. I'd ordered them. What's a word for giving up cakes? An *abdicaketion*.

She looked away from me and lifted the tray off the counter. I stared hungrily at what lay upon it and evaluated the transportability of each item. The green tea and espresso, not practical. I would spill almost all of either as I ran. The strawberry shortcake, too crumbly. The neenish tart would hold its shape, but it was too small. The lemon meringue pie was too squishy, but it was the biggest.

Before she could whisk it away, I leaned forward, grabbed it and ran off, stuffing some of it into my mouth while more of it disintegrated in my squeezing hand, leaving a trail of debris in my tracks. There was a commotion behind me, but I didn't look back. I would have laughed out loud, but it probably would've choked me, I had so much cake in my mouth. I felt exhilarated, or at least I thought I felt that way. It was more like I could see myself feeling elated, as if I was watching a movie in which I was the main character, a hilarious, dysfunctional, impulsive and unpredictable woman, stealing and eating cake on the run.

I don't remember going home, but I must have done, because I was there, sitting on my bed and playing Brahms on my violin at double speed so that I thought momentarily my crazy playing might saw the instrument in half. Robert looked in on me for a while, but left without a word—he knows that I don't like to be disturbed when I play the violin. At some point, Stef called to say dinner was ready. I can't remember what it was, or even if I went downstairs to eat at all, I was enjoying my music so much.

The evening wore on, and Robert and Stef made it clear that they were not enjoying it as much as I was. I guess

I'd been playing for over four hours by that time, and I'd completely memorised two long pieces by Brahms that evening. I'd slowed down to play at normal speed, but I'd astonished myself with how easily I was able to learn and recite the pieces with minimal practise. I'd never done that before. But now, I was even spotting ways in which the music could be improved, and I introduced my own distinctive tweaks to accomplish this.

Stef appeared at my door in her dressing gown, with a towel wrapped around her hair. "Chloe, I have to go to work tomorrow," she said, raising her voice so I could hear it over the stanzas I was playing.

"I know," I replied.

"What I mean is that I need to sleep now."

"Good night, then."

"Stop playing the violin, please! I'm going to bed now."

I gazed at her defiantly, increased the tempo of the drawing of the bow across my instrument and smiled.

"Chloe! What's got into you? You know it's a house rule that you don't play the violin after eleven at night. Ooh! I'd go and stay at my boyfriend's house, if he hadn't moved to Australia to get away from the quakes."

She pulled the door closed. I'm almost sure she stomped down the hall, but I couldn't see her, and nor could I hear her feet thumping over my playing; it was just the impression I had. I glanced at the clock. 11.23 p.m. Much later than I'd expected. Time had flown; not literally, of course, but it had passed more quickly than I'd realised.

I stopped playing and laid the violin down beside me on the duvet while I got undressed and put on a blue cotton nightie and a pair of fluffy purple slippers. They were Marinda's, as I didn't have any nightwear of my own anymore and, though they weren't my choice of apparel, I had no other dressing option. I didn't feel like going to bed yet, however, and I paced up and down in my room for a while.

What to do? What to do? I puzzled, shaking my head in a figure-eight pattern. I wasn't the least bit tired. In fact, I had heaps of energy, and I needed a way to release it. I was horny too.

No light seeped from under Robert's closed door. He had probably already gone to sleep. I didn't remember him saying goodnight to me, but he probably saw I was too busy with my music. Or perhaps I hadn't noticed him. I'm not sure. Putting aside the question I'd immediately formed about how he could sleep while I played the violin, yet Stef was adamant she could not, I entered his room with only the sound of my hot breath and beating heart in my ears.

He was lying on his back in bed, asleep, with earmuffs on. That solved the mystery of why my music hadn't disturbed him. I took off my slippers and nightie and placed them neatly up against the wall by the door. Then I turned and dived full-length onto the bed.

"I'm yours, lover boy!" I cried out as one of the pillows exploded in a cloud of feathers.

Robert jolted upright. "What! What's happening?" he blustered, taking deep breaths and clutching at his chest.

I didn't answer. I just lay prone on the bed, stark naked, my head leaning on one hand supported by the elbow, grinning at him saucily, surrounded by floating feathers.

He swept the earmuffs off his head. "Chloe! You startled me! What are you doing?"

"I would have thought that was obvious," I said, throwing my free arm around him and rolling over to rest snugly against him. "I'm not tired, and you're hot tonight. And I'm not referring to the temperature."

"I thought you'd lost interest in making love after the earthquake."

"Well, I'm interested now. Let's get on with it!"

Robert acquiesced, though, in fact, I gave him little choice as I climbed on top of him. Our sex was incredible—better than any other time I could remember. Exhausted and spent, Robert lay back, gasping for breath. I was equally breathless but had no shortage of energy. I felt as if there was an itch over my whole body that I had to scratch, yet couldn't, and it was driving me to be active. I slipped out of bed and put my nightie and slippers back on.

"Wait," puffed Robert. "Aren't you going to sleep with me tonight? I mean, have actual sleep?"

"No, my head's buzzing. I'm not tired. I'm going out for a walk."

"It's late, Chloe."

"I won't go far. Don't worry."

I went downstairs, but not before grabbing my violin on the way. I just felt like taking it with me. Maybe I could play it outside, seeing as my playing it in my room so late at night had annoyed Stef. When I reached the kitchen, I found Stef in there, dressed in a thin cotton dressing gown, eating a bowl of cornflakes. She glared at me as I made my entrance.

"Do you have to be so noisy?" she said.

"I haven't been playing," I said, gesturing with the violin as if it could explain its silence better than I could.

"I didn't mean that. Hey, where are you going?"

"Out for a walk," I said and quickly let myself out of the house.

It was mild outside, and clear. Above me, the canopy of stars in the Southern Hemisphere sky glittered and twinkled, brighter than I'd ever seen them. Perhaps there was less ambient light than usual from streetlights and neighbouring houses. Stunned, I gaped at the night sky before setting off down the driveway and onto the footpath, giving full throttle to Brahms on my violin.

Chapter Six

I've been playing the violin since I was six, and now I'm pretty good at it. When I was a child, though, I hated it because I couldn't make the sounds with it that I wanted. Everything came out as a blood-curdling shriek, like a cat clawing a blackboard. In those days, my parents were determined and patient. They also wore earmuffs when I practised. And my father kept paying for lessons until I improved.

Now I play whenever the mood takes me. I find recreating idyllic music is calming and relaxing; it immerses me in the experience and takes me into myself. I don't hate it any longer, of course, and now I wonder: do I love playing the violin? Can you love doing something like this? I think so. But if I have to ask myself this question, and don't just feel it like I feel the love for Robert, then do I love it truly? What would I forego if I had to give up something so I could play the violin?

I love reading music. The patterns of notes are so aesthetically pleasing, so mathematically balanced. They sing to me as I read them. And then I memorise them so I don't need the music sheets anymore, and I can reproduce the sounds on my violin whenever I choose. It's such a powerful feeling having such control over this art.

I love the feel of my violin, and what it does for me. It's

loyal and reliable and constant, like a good book. When I take it out of its case, my heartbeat quickens with anticipation. I love the touch and smell of the wood. I love the feel of the strings under my fingers and the vibrations that resonate through my jaw, shoulder and neck as I play. I love its extraordinary range of tonal sounds. It's simply fantastic to be physically part of such exquisite music.

When I am playing, I connect with my violin as if it's an extension of me. When I play music, it's as if I'm a storyteller, and I'm telling a story with elegant, passionate melody. It makes me feel happy or sad, and those feelings come out in the music, so I can share them with others. And sometimes the notes are so beautiful, so pure, each one cuts into me like a dagger of ice, and the music runs from my eyes.

I walked through the streets of Linwood, playing the most beautiful music I'd ever managed to play. Unfortunately, some of the residents did not like Brahms, or did not care for my unique interpretation of it, or perhaps they just did not appreciate me playing it after midnight outside their homes.

I made my way through the quiet residential streets, and lights came on in some of the houses as I went by. At one point, a brawny man in a singlet leaned out of his open window and shouted "Shuddupp, will you! It's hard enough trying to sleep with the bloody aftershocks every night without having to listen to the likes of you!" He slammed the window closed, drowning out my reply, which I doubt he would have wanted to hear anyway. He wasn't the only one, either. Other people demanded that I desist or go away or, preferably, both. They swore at me and I swore back at them before carrying on.

I headed west, towards the central city, though why I did that, I didn't know. No one could enter the central city anymore because of the military cordon around it. It was a dangerous place since the earthquake, with dozens of buildings unstable and awaiting demolition, off limits to everyone without a military or engineer escort. Nevertheless, I walked in that direction, playing a Concerto in D major, accompanied only by the occasional rumbling of the persistent aftershocks.

I passed by the ruins of abandoned corner shops that had partially crumbled during the quake and were no longer safe to be inhabited. The damage was worse as I drew closer to the CBD, because the buildings there were so much older and were constructed before the stricter buildings standards laws had been developed. I pondered two things in particular as I walked and played my violin. First, I thought that if an earthquake of the same magnitude had occurred in, say, London or Paris, there would be almost nothing left of those magnificent, but old, cities, whereas nearly all of the modern buildings in Christchurch had withstood the brutal ground acceleration. The other thing I thought about was the acronym CBD was clearly jumbled. BCD would obviously be a better-ordered choice.

It was dark, but I could make out the outlines of a man standing at the perimeter of the cordon at Madras Street. The poking-out bit of his silhouette had the unmistakable shape of a large gun. A soldier.

I walked up to him, finishing the last few bars of music as I reached the barrier in a well-timed finale.

"You can't pass this point, miss," he said.

"I know. I just wanted to—to see it, I guess."

"Are you all right, miss?"

"Of course I am. Why wouldn't I be? I feel great. I've

had a fantastic evening. I've made love with my boyfriend, I've been playing my favourite music, and I'm enjoying a lovely walk in the cool night air under the stars."

The soldier looked me up and down. "In your nightie and your fluffy slippers. With a violin."

I looked him up and down in return. "I like a man in uniform," I heard myself say. Why I said that, I don't know. It just seemed to come out of my mouth.

"Well, miss, that's good, because there's a couple more on the way for you." With the hand that wasn't caressing his weapon, he brought a walkie-talkie up to his face and spoke into it. "Send a police unit to cordon point fourteen."

"Hey! That's not necessary! I'm not doing anything wrong!"

"It's for your own safety, miss. The police officers will take you home. By the way, your playing was beautiful. Your pizzicato was exquisite."

"Oh, thank you! I like a man with a gun who appreciates classical music." I flashed my eyes at him and reached out to stroke the barrel of his gun, but he repositioned it out of my reach. My flirting seemed to know no boundaries this evening.

"Have you been drinking, miss? Or taking drugs?"

Before I could answer in the negative, a police car arrived at the scene. A large, bushy-eyebrowed man stepped out, along with a younger, smaller female officer. I recognised both of them from previous incidents I'd been involved in.

"Oh, not you again!" complained the bushy-eyebrowed sergeant, chewing on gum. "You're not out looking for your bloody cat again, are you?"

"No, I'm not looking for Sex at all. We haven't seen her since the earthquake. Someone else is probably looking after her now. I don't think she'll be here. I was just out for a walk."

The soldier looked at me oddly. The policewoman explained, "She has a cat called Sex who goes missing occasionally."

"Strange name," said the soldier.

"But no one ever forgets it!" I pointed out.

"Let us take you home, Ms Wilson," sighed the sergeant, gesturing towards the patrol car. "Are you still living at the same address in Riccarton, or have you had to move because of the earthquake?"

"I've moved." I told him Marinda's address.

They kindly drove me there, but they wouldn't let me play my violin on the way. It was 1.14 a.m. when I got home, and only then did I realise that I didn't have my keys with me. Luckily, there were lights on in the kitchen. Perhaps Robert or Stef had got up for a late-night snack. I rapped on the door with my bow and waited. Moments later, Stef pulled the door open. Curiously, she was dressed in her running sweats.

"Chloe! Where have you been? We've been worried about you."

"I'm fine. I just went for a walk. What's the big deal? Anyway, if you were worried, you would have come after me, wouldn't you?"

"I wasn't going to run down the road after you in my dressing gown. I woke Robert, and we went out looking for you after we'd got dressed, but we couldn't find you. We could hear you though. Probably everyone in Linwood could hear you playing that bloody fiddle of yours."

"Yeah, well, I didn't really think about that."

"And we tried calling you, but you didn't answer. Only when we got home did we discover your phone here on the kitchen table."

This discussion went on for a while, but it was mostly one-sided and consisted of Stef demanding in several variations what the bloody hell did I think I was doing. I tried to keep my answers short, partly because I couldn't actually explain it myself, and partly because her interrogation didn't make any sense to me, because I knew that Stef had wanted to go to bed much earlier, so why was she up now, at 1.30 in the morning, remonstrating with me? After a while, Robert came home, and we started the whole thing again. Frustrated, I ended the conversation myself after a while, telling them both to go and get some sleep, and went upstairs.

It was 3.30 a.m. before I finally crashed for the night though, and when I say night, I meant only until 5.45 a.m., as that was when I got up again. I couldn't sleep because my brain was so busy talking to itself.

I'd been busy. While I had been walking, I'd also been thinking about the post-quake state of Christchurch, how the CBD (I will always think of it as the BCD) is twisted and broken, as are some of the eastern suburbs. Then, I thought, why does Christchurch have so many suburbs? And why do they all seem to overlap? While the post office thinks a particular street is in one suburb, local real estate agents put it in another (more expensive) suburb. The residents have their own ideas about this too. It's not uncommon for a particular house to 'belong' to three or even four different suburbs.

That irked me because it was clearly muddled organisation, and that's one thing I can't stand. I like things to be black and white, not shades of grey. I didn't even know if Marinda's house was in the suburb of Linwood, Phillipstown or Richmond. And while I'd been walking and thinking, this had bothered me more and more. With my perseverative thinking, it's hard to let go of things like this.

So at about 2.00 a.m., I pulled out an old street map of Christchurch that I'd found in one of Marinda's drawers, and grabbed some highlighter pens. I spread the map on the floor in my room, lay down next to it and got to work. For a laugh, I started by scribbling 'hobbits' on one side, then filled in the other sides with 'elves', 'dwarves' and 'orcs'.

This gave me an idea, and I tried superimposing a map of Middle Earth over the Christchurch one, but despite how creatively I rotated it, there was no close match. Giving up on that, I wondered if I could simply draw a zodiac around the city, centred by the CBD, with main roads denoting the borders and naming each suburb after the constellation that covered it, but decided that was unsatisfactory as it would lead to peculiar, and unworkable, pie-slice-shaped suburbs.

After half an hour, I stopped tinkering with unconventional solutions like these and began a process of rationalisation and elimination. The problem was simply that there are too many suburbs, I decided, and no one knows exactly where the borders are. I began demarcating areas with my highlighter pens. The CBD (which, of course, I would rename the BCD) and Hagley Park were obvious sections. Around those, I drew a rough circle, following the ring road most of the way, but extending to the hills on the south side. This part I divided into six segments. After that, I marked a few arterial roads leading away from the city, added a few more lines, and I was done. The only thing remaining was to assign the names.

Before posting the plan of these proposed new suburbs on my website and submitting it to the Mayor, I felt that I should put considerable thought into giving them proper monikers. So, in the next half hour, I devoted myself to this purpose. I oscillated between the ideas of coming up with completely new names and reusing some of the old names. If I reused some of the old ones, I could prefix them with 'New', for instance, 'New Linwood'. They might even retain these labels for hundreds of years, like 'New College' in Oxford. But New Brighton was a sticking point. It was already 'New'. Could it be 'New New Brighton'? I soon determined that was a ridiculous idea and simply wrote down the original names of some of the suburbs, leaving out the ones I didn't like.

Finished, I studied my work, pleased with myself. The map was a mess of creases and fluorescent ink, but it would provide city planners with a blueprint for *resuburbising* Christchurch. I threw the map and all my sketches and notes into a box and put it by my door so I wouldn't forget to post it tomorrow. That would be expensive; probably enough to give me *postage traumatic stress disorder*. But it would all be worth it if they built a statue of me or something.

I went to bed, my head buzzing with new ideas. Tomorrow, I would plan the redesign of the whole city, post-quake. That should keep me busy for the afternoon. Unless something more interesting comes up, of course.

At 5.45 a.m., an aftershock—probably a 'four'—woke me, and I got up, feeling full of energy, despite having only two and a quarter hours' sleep. I dressed and went downstairs to the kitchen, where I paced up and down restlessly while I waited for the water to boil over the little gas-powered stove, which seemed to take forever. My mind seemed to be racing as fast as my feet as I walked back and forth until, finally out of patience, I switched it off, left the house (making sure I remembered my bag this time) and set off for

McDonald's for an early breakfast.

I expected that once the Mayor saw my plans for the redesign of Christchurch (which, I reminded myself, I would finish that afternoon), I was bound to be given a top position in supervising the rebuild of the city. I would also update everyone following my blog with these plans as well as all my usual stuff, which tended to be my random thoughts of the day and what I had been eating. One million followers might be attainable, and then I could sell it to Google or Apple or someone.

I wasn't even half-way to McDonald's before I'd decided to give up university for good. There was just too much else for me to do, and I was thinking so clearly and imaginatively now. Ideas flooded my mind, saturating it with so many thoughts that I lost myself amongst them. I decided to write a novel, which I expected would be a bestseller, of course. I didn't know exactly what I would write about, but it must be easy as thousands of books are published every month, though I did know I would write speculative fiction. My mind was so full of crazy ideas that they couldn't help but come through in my writing.

Giving up my medication had been an awesome idea. I hadn't felt better for ages. I had so much energy, and my mind was on fire with creative thoughts.

I had a muffin and four coffees for breakfast. I was getting used to coffee now, and wished I'd taken up the habit a long time ago because having a coffee at a café is such a cool thing to do. Afterwards, I walked home, my head buzzing. I'd become a real *caffiend*.

Robert and Stef were having their breakfast at the kitchen table.

"Hi, you two," I said, startling them as I bustled in.

Stef looked up at me with droopy eyes, a coffee cup

half-way to her mouth. "Where have you been? Have you slept at all?"

"Sure, I did. For two and a quarter hours. I don't need much sleep at the moment. I got up early, and I've been out for a walk."

"Well, I'm exhausted after being kept awake by your late-night antics, and I've got to walk to work today, so I'm not happy, Chloe."

"It didn't bother me," added Robert. Stef shot him a glance Medusa would be proud of.

"It didn't bother me either," I said.

Stef frowned. "Are you sure you're all right, Chloe?"

"Yes, I feel great. I'm over the earthquakes, and I'm not obsessed with the quake stats any longer. I've thought of more interesting things to do. I'm going to come up with a redesign of Christchurch and submit it to the Mayor, and I'm going to give up university, and I'm going to write a bestseller, and—"

"Hey, what was that?"

"I'm going to write a bestseller," I repeated.

"No, wait. Go back. The bit about giving up university. Where did that come from?" asked Stef.

"Well, obviously, I'll have to do that. I'll be far too busy with everything else to carry on studying."

"But what about your psychology degree? That's what you've wanted to do for the past two years. Why give up now?"

"They can't teach me anything that I can't find out by myself," I heard myself say. "I can learn what I need by skimming the textbooks. And I'm not going to have time for lectures. Don't worry about me. I think I know what I'm doing, but if turns out that I don't know, I'm sure I will be able to figure it out. I really want to do these things, to do something important. I'm tired of muddling around as a student. So I'm going to start writing a fantastic bestseller."

"What makes you think you can write a bestseller?" demanded Stef. "Apart from your university essays, you've never written anything longer than a shopping list."

"I'm going to buy heaps of books about writing bestsellers. I'll read them, and then I'll just do it. Obviously." I heard myself rudely snapping out these words staccato fashion. I don't know if it was because I was angry or simply becoming impatient or bored with Stef's questioning. Or maybe because at the back of my mind, there was a quiet voice telling me these ideas of mine were all crazy. My inner critic, from whom I hadn't heard much for a couple of days. I mentally silenced it. It was holding me back from pursuing my dreams.

"What are you going to write about?" asked Robert.

That stumped me. I gawked at him for a few moments, or one long moment, I don't really know, as I don't know how long a moment is, exactly. But then I blurted out, "About me, of course!"

"Um... why would that be a bestseller?"

"Because!" I said, and stomped upstairs, leaving them to ponder over my vague and unsatisfying explanation. I had work to do.

How hard could it be to write a bestseller? I didn't know. To find out, I bought a heap of ebooks about writing bestsellers so I could read them on my laptop, which was still the only thing in the house that had power, thanks to my hooking it up to the rooftop solar panel. I spent hours skimming through fourteen of these 'how-to' books and encountered so many contradictions that I decided I'd learned nothing, apart from learning I'd wasted my money. Oh well. I could always self-publish my journal as a wacky fictional memoir of a young woman with Asperger's Syndrome and Bipolar Disorder.

I was tiring of that idea, though, and I was already bored with my master plan to redesign Christchurch. I don't know why, but I just couldn't seem to focus on anything at present. And everything around me seemed to be happening in slow motion, which made it all even more tedious and frustrating, and that's why I'd sought refuge in my room. There, I could immerse myself in my own thoughts, and they could arrive at any rate they chose. Indeed, they continued to flood my mind, and I kept pacing up and down across my room, even while reading.

Another thought hit me, a tangent to a tangent to a tangent. During my research into writing bestsellers, I'd read a passage about handling time travel in fiction. There are a few different variants authors use, and they have their literary advantages and drawbacks. It's a kind of genre fiction that I've always liked, ever since reading H.G. Wells' *The Time Machine* as a little girl and spending many *insomniacal* hours imagining building such a device and travelling back and forth to visit interesting times. Though I realised I couldn't know which periods in the future would be the interesting ones, so I'd have to guess.

Recently, I'd read a romantic suspense time-travel story, *The Ruby Brooch*, and I'd once again been fascinated by the idea of escaping the present and visiting the past. Now that I'd read a few pages on how to write such a story, I began to wonder, not about writing of time travel, but of achieving it somehow. After all, I'd managed to redeploy the solar panel on the roof to power my laptop and the modem after reading a short article about powering laptops on long desert excursions. If I read about quantum physics, maybe I could create a device to send myself back in time, and power it from my laptop with a USB cable. I'd seen it done in the movies, and while those contraptions clearly weren't real, no one appeared to think they would be overly complicated to make. How hard could it be to build a time machine?

I could warn people about the earthquake. I could find Marinda and save her.

I decided to ask Robert what he thought of my idea.

"Robert?" I called out. If he was in his room, he should hear me. No reply came, so I went looking for him. I passed his empty room and went downstairs, but he was not there either. I looked outside and finally spotted him walking along the footpath a few houses away towards the local port-a-loo. Many parts of the city where there was still no running water had sprouted these portable toilets as street furniture. This particular one was our preferred means of personal waste disposal because we'd grown weary of digging new holes in the garden.

I hurried towards the port-a-loo, eager to talk to Robert and too impatient to wait for his return. By the time I reached it, a young woman in a blue sweatshirt waited outside, tapping her foot and adjusting her sunglasses. I walked past her and rapped on the blue plastic port-a-loo door.

"Hey, Robert!"

"Excuse me," said Blue Sweatshirt Woman, "there's a queue here. I'm next."

"I'm not pushing in. I don't want to have a pee, I want to talk to my boyfriend, so excuse me! Robert? Can you hear me?"

"Yes, Chloe, what is it?" came the muffled sound of

Robert's voice from the other side of the plastic door.

"I've got an idea I want to talk to you about!" I shouted, hoping he could hear me clearly if I spoke up.

"Can't you wait four minutes?"

"No, I can't!" *What a stupid question.* Next to me, Blue Sweatshirt Woman stood with her arms crossed, tapping her foot in sets of three. This wasn't stimming; I think she was impatient rather than anxious.

"What is it?" said Robert, punctuating his question with other sounds.

"Can you help me work out how to build a time machine?"

Robert replied, but I couldn't make out what he said because Blue Sweatshirt woman scoffed loudly at the same time. "It's a freaking port-a-loo, not a Tardis. It doesn't go anywhere, and it's definitely no bigger on the inside than it looks on the outside. You're nuts if you think you can travel through time in a port-a-loo powered by crap."

"I don't mean this thing," I snapped. "Mind your own fucking business. I'm trying to have a conversation with my boyfriend. Well, Robert? Any ideas?"

"Not from in here. Just wait a bit, will you?"

I huffed in annoyance. Blue Sweatshirt Woman smiled at me. I didn't know why, and it only irritated me further.

"Can you just tell me if it's even theoretically possible?" I said, rapping on the blue plastic.

I heard the toilet flushing. There was no other response.

"I think that's a 'no'," said Blue Sweatshirt Woman. "But you could always try the chemical toilet in the next street. It might have more gas."

I turned, ready to growl at her, but at that moment,

Robert stepped out of the port-a-loo, grabbed my hand and started to walk home. Blue Sweatshirt Woman stepped inside, grinning at me as she shut the door. I followed Robert, tethered to him.

"Theoretically, I think it might be possible," said Robert after a while. We were already halfway home.

"Really?" I hugged him tightly. "You'll help me? Wow! That's fantastic! Do you really think we can do it?"

"No, probably not. But we'll know in a minute."

"In a *minute*? How? How will you know in a minute if it's possible?"

"That's simple, Chloe. Just promise me this: if we manage to build a working time machine, will you go back in time to earlier this morning and leave the design plans under the front door mat?"

"Uh—yeah, I suppose I can do that. Why?"

"Because," said Robert as we rounded the gate and started up the garden path, "now all we have to do is look under the mat and see if they're there. If they are, then obviously at some point in the future we succeeded, and now we'll have the design plans to actually build the thing. But if there's nothing there, then clearly we will never manage to do it because you will never come back to leave the plans for us to find, and in that case, we may as well not bother trying."

"Oh." That sounded like it made sense in a Robert-like logical way, but I'm not sure I truly got it. Even so, I lifted the welcome mat with a heightened sense of expectation.

There was nothing under it.

"Shit." I burst into tears, surprising myself at my sudden emotion. "I wanted to save Marinda. I wanted to save everyone."

"I know," said Robert, guiding me inside, his arm around my shoulders.

CHAPTER SEVEN

Bipolar Disorder is awesome.
   I hate it.

I paced back and forth in my room for an hour, clenching my fists, kicking at the carpet, my thoughts stampeding in my head. I didn't know what was going on with me. It was like having the PMTs of a dozen periods, what I call a *menstrosity*, an internal itch as if I'd been snorting thistles, and the racing mind of an insomniac on speed all at once, cramming me mercilessly into my own overcrowded head. My mind had turned into a racetrack of disconnected thoughts, all vying for my attention at the same time, so I couldn't focus on anything, and yet couldn't avoid them either. I felt as if I were rushing headlong downhill, almost out of control, frightened, yet elated at the same time. I didn't know where I would end up, and it actually felt exhilarating.

   I guessed it was because I'd stopped my medication, or rather that I hadn't had my prescription refilled after losing my pills in our old destroyed house. I was held firmly in the grip of a bipolar hypomanic episode, and in danger of becoming fully manic. But it was too late for me now to alter course. I'd become addicted to the flood of ideas, to the soaring energy I possessed, to my seemingly rampant sexuality and endless horny thoughts, to the personal power I felt I had, to my free-running imagination. There seemed to be nothing that I couldn't conceive or do, and I loved feeling like this. Though some small, quiet part of me knew that I needed help, I knew I wasn't going to ask for it. I'd take this trip to the end, wherever it takes me, even though I knew from experience it was likely to end with a slump.

I went downstairs for a drink of water. I was alone in the house now. Robert may have gone to university, or maybe he was just down the road at the port-a-loo again. I fetched a glass from the cupboard, placed it on the counter top and pulled open the pantry door. We kept our bottled water in there, as it was the coolest spot. I didn't like drinking water heated by the sun, so we always kept it in the shade.

"Shit!"

All the bottled water had gone. Six empty 2L plastic bottles lay on the pantry floor. I slammed the pantry door. I checked our back-up supply in the hall, but the containers there hadn't been replenished either. They were stacked up in a small triangle, three containers high, and I scattered them with a single kick. It had been Robert's turn to take them down to the water tanker, but he obviously hadn't done it. Maybe he'd forgotten. Maybe he was too busy and planned to do it later. Maybe he was just too fucking lazy. I felt furious. If he'd been there, I would have screamed at him. Instead, I had to yell at an empty house.

But that didn't help relieve my thirst. I realised that I should fetch the water, but I didn't feel like doing that. Instead, I charged out of the house, forgetting to close the front door, let alone lock it. I'd go and buy some bottled water, just for me. That would teach him to forget to fetch the water when it was his turn.

I was vaguely aware of a voice (mine, but somewhat quieter than usual) in the back of my head insisting that I should take all of the bottles and containers down to the water tanker myself and fill them up because we would all need water later that day for cooking, drinking and brushing our teeth. I paused in the front yard and glanced at the supermarket trolley we'd temporarily appropriated for that purpose, which we kept hidden when we weren't using it behind some shrubbery.

No, I decided, Robert can do that. It's his turn, after all. I rationalised that I shouldn't have to take the rattly, wobbly old thing down to the tanker when it wasn't my turn.

I walked to the nearest dairy, which was on a corner four blocks away. A small wall outside the corner shop had collapsed, and the bricks had been stacked up next to where it had stood in low, loose stacks. Inside the shop, a large plywood board covered up one window that had obviously been broken but not fixed yet. There were always little reminders of the earthquake, wherever I went.

It was dark inside the shop because it didn't have power either. Enough sunlight filtered in for me to see the chiller cabinet was barren. I cursed softly, and then turned to face the proprietor, an old Chinese woman barely taller than the counter.

"Do you have any bottled water?"

"Sorry, love," she replied, her voice whistling between gaps in her teeth, creating an effect that, combined with her accent, made her words almost unintelligible to me. "All ran out. You try again tomorrow. Or maybe you could try Patel's, three streets over." She jabbed her hand to indicate the direction I should walk.

I left the dairy and quickly walked on to Patel's Dairy, becoming thirstier and grumpier with each step as the summer morning sun beat down on me. I hadn't remembered to bring a hat or apply sunscreen, so I was probably going to get sunburnt, but at that point, even though I was aware of the possibility, I didn't care much. I just wanted to get some water. And some hokey pokey ice cream too. A double scoop in a cone would do.

Patel's dairy looked as if a swarm of starving and parched locusts had raided it. There was no bottled water or soft drinks, no ice cream and certainly no power either. I hadn't stopped to think that, without power, all the ice cream in the local shops would have melted by now. Mr Patel smiled sheepishly at me and gestured towards the rest of his produce, most of which was far from fresh, and at his shelves, where a few cans of tinned food sat, unwanted. Spam. Ox tongue in brine. Chestnut mushrooms in oil.

I left, thinking the situation was ridiculous. All I wanted was a bottle of water. But, after the quake, people had been out panic-buying the stuff. It seemed no one had any left.

Perhaps I should have pushed the trolley down to the water tanker and replenished our containers after all, I thought. But now it was too late for that. I was on a mission, and I wouldn't let anything deter me from my goal of a bottle of water and a double-scoop hokey pokey ice cream. Aspies don't abort missions—I certainly don't, anyway. I keep going. It's my perseverative behaviour again.

I walked on, now hot and frustrated, but not ready to give up. There must be a bottle of water somewhere in Christchurch, I rationalised, and I intended to find it. I must have gone at least three kilometres by now and, thankfully, I could see another dairy up ahead, a small corner shop topped with a giant Coca-Cola hoarding. I marched towards it. I wasn't myself at all; I felt stressed and disassociated somehow, like I was shadowing a desperate person, and that desperate person was me. It was confusing and intriguing at the same time. In the back of my mind, I knew that something wasn't right, yet I still didn't care. It was like I was watching myself in a movie for which the scriptwriters were insane, and I didn't care how the main character (me) felt, and didn't think of the consequences of whatever would happen next.

Some kids next door to the dairy played some kind of war game, or cops and robbers or something like that, running, shouting and laughing. I stared at them for a moment, thinking them crazy for running around in this heat, though I was aware of the irony that I still had to walk home, and I'd probably be as red as a lobster when I got there because I hadn't applied any sunscreen. I glanced at the name above the fly screen door as I went in. It said 'Carlos's Corner Shop'.

A fat, sweaty, unshaven man with traces of ice cream around his mouth sat behind the counter, a *slubberdegullion* if I ever saw one. It appeared this part of the city fortunately had power. A small television showed The Poker World Series, and the man twirled a small bracelet of beads in one hand as he watched. He looked up when the bell rang behind me to alert him that someone had entered the shop. He wiped his mouth, and his face cracked open with a wide grin as he lurched to his feet.

"Ah, young lady, thank you for gracing my humble establishment with your visit. I do not remember seeing you here before. You are a new customer, no?"

"No. I mean, yes." His charming words flummoxed me. *Is he like this to all of his female customers?*

"Ah, *né*, I was sure of it. Carlos would not forget a face as pretty as yours. I would not. Now, how can I be of service to you?" He raised his eyebrows and shook his head from side to side. I didn't know what that gesture meant. It was

Greek to me.

"Do you have any bottled water?"

"Ah..." It seemed impossible for his smile to broaden further, but it did, nevertheless. "The charming young lady with the blue patch of hair is in luck. You are. I have remaining just two bottles of the finest mineral water available for purchase anywhere in the world. And for you, my lovely young friend, one of them can be yours for only twenty-four dollars." His eyes twinkled at me as he gestured towards them in the drinks refrigerator beside the counter. "Or you can have both of them for fifty dollars, a real bargain."

"Twenty-four dollars for a bottle of water? That's outrageous!"

"Ah... I understand your reticence. They are expensive, yes... but they are the best mineral waters imported from Konitsa, in Greece. Finest quality." He leaned in closer to me. I could smell his sweat. "They may also be the last bottles of mineral water to be found in Christchurch."

I stared at him, holding my breath.

He moved away, flicking his beads nonchalantly. "Of course, there is free water at the tankers... but if you want the finest—"

"All right! I'll have one." My words came out sounding harsh. Maybe my throat was parched.

He beamed. "Excellent! You make me very happy. You do."

Reluctantly, I went to get my purse out of my bag, and only then, in horror, realised that I'd left it at home. Again.

"Shit! I've left my money at home. Can I pay you later?"

Carlos jerked his head up and clicked his tongue, an

expression of sadness on his face that even I could discern. "*Ochi*. Ah... I am so sorry, my pretty, young friend, but I cannot extend credit to anyone. That is beyond the pecuniary capabilities of a small businessman like me."

The irony of him declaring himself a 'small' businessman did not pass me by, but I did not comment on it. Instead, I pivoted about sharply and stomped out.

"Please, come again!" he called. "Bring your money next time!"

I seethed with anger, but had taken no more than two steps away from the dairy before one of the excited kids from next door, looking over his shoulder at the friend chasing him, barrelled straight into me, and knocked us both to the ground.

"Watch where you're bloody going!" I shouted at him, getting to my feet.

He scrambled up. "S-sorry," he blustered.

I ignored him, focussing my attention on the replica pistol he'd dropped. At first glance, it looked realistic. An idea occurred to me, but I didn't think through the consequences of it at all. I picked up the toy gun; or, rather, it was like watching a crime show on TV in which I saw myself pick it up. "Stay here!" I ordered the boy and his friend, who had come over.

"Hey! Where are you going?" said the boy. I didn't answer him, for I was already back in the shop. I marched up to the counter. Carlos was watching TV, one hand buried in a sweetie jar.

"Water! Now!" I demanded, holding the toy pistol at arm's length. It wobbled a bit, but it did point in his general direction.

He sat back, his eyebrows going up. He licked his lips,

withdrew his hand from the jar and said, "Ah... you've got to be bloody joking."

"I want that water. Hand it over now."

Carlos stared back at me and popped a couple of liquorice allsorts into his mouth. The only sound was the irritating click-clack of his beads as he flicked them with the other hand.

"Please." I may as well be polite.

Carlos leaned forward. "Beretta M9 pistol. Standard issue to US military personnel. How did my pretty, young friend obtain such a thing?"

"Never mind. Just give me the friggin' water." I barely recognised my own voice. It was as if I was listening to a distorted recording.

He shook his head slowly. "Ah... I bet the young lady's pistol is not even loaded."

"Water! Now!"

"You know, my pretty, young friend, I sold a toy gun remarkably similar to the one you have to the *paidiá,* the children, next door only yesterday." He stood up and stepped in front of the drinks refrigerator, blocking it entirely. There was no way I could get past him to snatch a bottle of his precious Greek water.

"Shit!" I turned around and ran out of the shop, his laughter ringing in my ears. I dropped the gun at the feet of the kids outside and ran around the corner. By now, I was crying, tears mingling with sweat in my eyes, so they stung. Halfway down the street, I stopped and turned around. No one had followed me.

I was hyperventilating. Or perhaps I was just really puffed out. Whatever; I should probably get more exercise in future. But what was I to do now?

I walked slowly back towards the dairy. I thought that I should apologise. But how? How does one apologise for what I'd just done? I paused outside the door. The kids had gone. Maybe to tell their parents. Maybe to call the police. Maybe to copy my behaviour and try to rob Patel's dairy a few streets away. I didn't know.

I'd stopped crying, but I had a massive headache and felt quite sick, as if I were developing a migraine. I was in no condition to walk home.

I poked my head around the edge of the shop door. Carlos was again engrossed in the World Series of Poker on TV. I took a pace forward. The bell rang as I stepped over the threshold, startling me. Carlos looked up, stared at me for a moment, then grinned widely and laughed.

"Um... sorry," I said, then backed out of the shop. God, I felt terrible. Tired and sick. And stupid. Yes, especially stupid. But I didn't feel like myself at all. It was as if someone had switched me onto maniacal autopilot, and I, the real me, was just along for the ride.

In the driveway next to the dairy stood a red Renault, gleaming as if it were new, though it obviously wasn't. It wasn't locked either, so I slipped inside. I knew what I had to do, for I'd looked up how to hot-wire a car on the internet once after seeing it done in a crime show on TV. Twenty seconds later, my tampering started the car, and I drove it unsteadily out of the driveway and back the way I'd come. At this point, I remembered that I didn't know how to drive. Luckily, the Renault was an automatic, and I vaguely knew what Stef does to make The Frog go, which was fiddling with the controls and moderately swearing. Anyway, I got the Renault moving, and I wasn't going far, so it probably didn't matter much that I wasn't driving it smoothly or even particularly straight. And, if I was lucky, Carlos wouldn't even know it was gone before I'd finished with it.

I drove waywardly, one minute laughing raucously at my audaciousness and the next minute sobbing with guilt and despair. I don't know how I made it back alive, but somehow I did. I left the car parked on Linwood Ave and decided to walk home from there.

First, though, I found a public phone booth and dialled the police. I'd always wanted to do this. It rang twice before someone picked it up.

"Christchurch Police. How can I help you?"

"Hi, I want to report the whereabouts of a stolen car."

"Hang on, miss. How do you know it was stolen?" asked the female voice at the other end.

"I stole it. Now it's parked on Linwood Ave." I gave her the registration number and the car's exact position.

There was a pause. "Thank you for reporting that, miss. Now, just for the record, to who am I speaking?"

"Oh, my name. Yes, it's—"

I hung up at that point and walked home. Then I did what I should have done in the first place. I collected up all the empty water bottles we had, put them into the shopping trolley we'd temporarily appropriated, and walked down to the water tanker to refill them, before coming home.

It was the nicest water I'd ever tasted.

It was early afternoon by now, and I decided to take a shower. This was no ordinary domestic task in these times as our area still had no running water. I gathered the things I would need and headed towards the communal showers on the corner of Wainoni and Breezes Road. That was quite a walk, but I didn't mind as I still had plenty of energy.

The showers were in cubicles aboard a flat-bed truck.

At busy times, there were often queues to access them; friendly locals would line up with their towels and toiletries and chat to each other. I didn't like chatting to strangers, so I usually went there when I thought there would not be many people. Luckily, today, in the late morning, it was quiet.

I'd just put my foot on the first metal stair, ready to mount them, when a pair of tanned, jandaled feet, the hairiness of which would rival a hobbit's, came into view at my eye level. Startled, I stepped back with an audible 'oh' and looked up.

"Hey, I didn't mean to give you a fright," said the man, as he descended the steps, blue towel and toiletry bag curled in his arms. He wore walking shorts, and instead of dressing in his white tee-shirt, he'd tucked it into the top of his shorts, so he was bare chested.

Abstract tattoos adorned both of his upper arms. I stared at his muscular physique and then lifted my eyes to his face. I'd seen him somewhere before, but I couldn't remember where. Gravity, or some other natural force, pulled my gaze downwards again.

"Hey, I remember you," he said. "You're the woman from the plane who sat next to me but had the wrong seat. Yeah, that was a shame. I ended up with that large woman sitting next to me. She wasn't any fun to talk to."

I wrenched my stare away from his rippling six-pack abs to look him directly in the face. He smiled broadly at me, and my heart missed a beat, my breath shortened, and I gasped.

"Looks as though you'll have the whole place to yourself," said the man, gesturing up the steps to where the cubicled showers waited on the flat-bed truck. He leaned forward, invading my personal space, so close we were almost touching. Usually, I would shrink away in horror from this, or even push the person away, but strangely, I didn't want to do that. I wanted to grab him and pull him even closer.

"I'm Angelo. I did introduce myself on the plane, but I don't suppose you remember that."

Angelo. An Italian name. No wonder he's so touchy-feely.

"Chloe," I heard myself squeak. The lower half of my body tingled. My horny thoughts reasserted themselves. A little voice in my mind screamed 'No', but it sounded as if it came from a long distance away. My quivering body silently cried 'Yes'.

"I'm a barista at Café Gorgon. That's nearby. Do you know it? What do you do?"

"Um... yes, I know where that café is.... I'm a student. Or was. I don't know anymore."

"Cool. Well, I'll see you around," said Angelo. He brushed my arm with his as he stepped past. The touch of his skin against mine sent jolts of pleasure all over my body. I moaned.

"Are you all right?"

"Yes," I whispered. *No. I shouldn't do this. I shouldn't.*

"Okay, then. I should go," he replied, but he didn't move for several seconds. He just watched me.

"Wait." I drew closer to him, running my hand over his muscled, hairy chest.

We had sex in the showers, wild, rapid, wet and almost entirely standing up. It lasted only a few minutes; I'm not sure how long exactly because I'd taken my watch off. But it was quick. Then Angelo pulled on his shorts and jandals, smiled at me and left without another word.

I showered, talking to myself as the water cascaded over my body. I didn't even know how I felt about what I'd just done. How would I tell Robert? And Stef? Aspies generally don't lie (can't lie, perhaps), but is withholding the truth lying or not?

My mind raced almost too fast for me to formulate these questions, let alone consider and answer them. These thoughts lasted only a few moments. Robert would almost certainly never find out if I didn't tell him. I decided that it didn't matter anyway; all that was important was how I felt at the moment.

I finished showering, dressed and walked home, confused, high as a kite and still feeling horny.

Robert had left for university when I got home. He'd left a note on the table saying how much he loved me, and that he hoped I was feeling better. I left it there and went upstairs to my room, intending to start writing my book. My laptop was still running off the solar-powered battery, and I had a flaky internet connection most of the time. There were rumours that power would be restored any day now, but the water would take longer. About time. I could hardly wait.

I typed feverishly for an hour and a half, writing pages of narrative about myself, my medical history, my psychiatric history and my education. I read through it all and couldn't decide if it was a masterly exposition or simply a tedious monologue. Even at this maniacal rate, I would exceed the ten days I had estimated it would take to write my bestseller. Writing must be harder than I thought, I concluded.

I went online to research psychotropic drugs to ensure I put the correct information in my book. At the back of my mind, my neglected inner critic piped up again, reminding me that I should see my doctor, that something was wrong, drastically wrong, with my mood state and my behaviour. I didn't listen. I'd been having too much fun to listen to that annoying inner voice anyway. Who needs it? Fuck it. I didn't.

After a while browsing some of the psychology sites I frequently visited, I started reading an article about addictions. Drugs. Gambling. Alcohol. Sex. It was quite fascinating. I'd been wondering if I was not addicted to my meds at all, and now I wondered if I'd become addicted to sex, and that might be the underlying reason for my uncharacteristic sexual misadventure earlier that day. But, according to the article, that wasn't my condition at all.

A pop-up distracted me. The browser must have been serving me ads based on keywords in the article, for it had displayed advertisements for cheap pharmaceuticals, sexual performance enhancing herbs and now online poker. I remembered playing poker last year with Robert and Stef and friends (well, not strictly friends as such, more like weirdos who happened to be staying with us at the time), and I had enjoyed it. Perhaps playing online wouldn't be quite as much fun as I probably wouldn't be taking my clothes off, but it might still be a laugh. I clicked on the pop-up and was taken to a poker website.

It turned out to be a pay site. Without further ado, and with even less thought, I deposited some money from my savings. I had plenty because I'd saved most of my share of what Robert and I had won last year. Two thousand dollars ought to be enough for the high-roller tables, at least to begin with. I had no expectation of losing it, or any part of it for that matter. I felt unbeatable. The possible negative consequences never entered my mind, nor the inadvisability of playing poker for money while I was undergoing a bipolar hypomanic episode. Although I'd only played the game once before, I remembered the rules, and I expected to win.

Thirsty, I grabbed a drink of water. I vaguely remembered that I hadn't eaten yet that day, or the night before, but I didn't feel hungry. Not for food, anyway. I had other raging appetites.

One of them was thrill seeking, and that's how I approached the game. I played with an avatar of a young woman with dyed hair, somewhat resembling myself, with the moniker 'Bipolar Girl'. It seemed to me that the other online players were too timid, betting cautiously and folding often. I played every round, bluffing when I held a lousy hand, betting outrageously whenever I thought I had a good one. Once I had a handful of those knobbly black things and won a heap of money. It wasn't long before I was two grand ahead and felt utterly invincible.

After a while, Carlos 'The Greek' started betting more aggressively against me, and I began to lose. Not much at first, just a few hundred. Then 'Pieter The Great' ganged up on me too. My bluffing was more like fluffing now. I lost hundreds more to 'Chen 10'. They weren't afraid of me anymore, but I fought on, defeat unthinkable, my mind racing, never losing confidence, yet becoming more desperate with each heavy loss.

Whenever I needed to, I deposited more money. I wasn't giving up! I endured yet another big loss to Carlos 'The Greek'. I needed to recover my money.

That's when my flaky internet connection went down.

I shrieked. I screamed. I jumped to my feet and kicked the glass, half-full of water, to the other side of the room, where it smashed against the wall. I fell to my knees, beating my hands on the floor in frustration, cursing like a sailor who's found the only brothel in port closed for renovations.

A light flickered on my laptop. The internet connection was back; unreliable, perhaps, but springing to an uncertain life like the fanned embers of a dying fire. I lay on the floor, mouse in hand, muttering at the laptop, trying to reconnect to the game.

"Chloe! What's going on?"

I looked at the door. Stef stood there. She must have returned from work. I had no idea how long I'd been playing the game. Unless she'd come home early, it must have been hours. I stared at her vacantly, slow to process the transition from the virtual world of the poker game to real life.

"Chloe! What's wrong? I heard glass smashing, and you screaming." I watched her look around the room, or rather, it felt like I was observing myself watch her look around the room. I felt somewhat disassociated.

I realised that Stef had spotted the broken glass against the wall. I returned my attention to my laptop, where I was back in the poker game.

"What the hell's going on? What are you doing?" She bent down next to me as I placed a $200 bet because I had a pair of fours.

"Don't worry, Stef. I'll win my money back. I feel lucky."

"Win it back? How much have you lost?"

"I'm not sure exactly. Five thousand. Or it might be seven thousand. Most of it to Carlos the friggin' Greek. I've been *cashtrated*!"

"Seven thousand dollars! Are you out of your mind? How long have you been gambling like this?"

"A few hours. Piss off, Stef. I'm busy."

"But why are you doing this, Chloe? What's got into

you?"

I sniggered at that last question. "Angelo, the Italian barista. I had sex with him in the showers."

"Chloe! This isn't like you. Hey, wait a minute... did you see your doctor about replacing the medications you lost in the earthquake?"

I cackled. Ah, the medications. The friggin' medications. I felt good. I felt as if I didn't need them anymore. And now...

"I feel fucking amazing," I said.

Stef grabbed my arm and hauled me to my feet. "Come on," she said. "Get in the car."

"Have you got The Frog back now?"

"Shit! No! I keep forgetting. I'm not used to being without it. Never mind, come downstairs. I'll call us a taxi."

"We're a taxi! We're a taxi!" I giggled, singing it off-key as Stef dragged me downstairs to the kitchen and sat me at the table.

"Stay there. I'll make you a green tea. Or a coffee." She picked up the phone and punched some numbers without taking her eyes off me.

"I wanted to build a time-travel machine this morning," I said, even as Stef made her phone calls. "I asked Robert to help me. He said it might be possible, but I'll never do it because I didn't send anything back in time to tell me how. That sucks. Anyway, you know, that doesn't matter anymore. I decided to write a bestseller instead. I told you about that already. But before that, I went to have a shower. I met Angelo there, at the communal showers. He's hot, seriously smoking hot. I couldn't help myself. Something compelled me to do it, to have sex with him. I'm sure Robert won't mind. He'll understand. And then I did some research and then some gambling—"

I remember Stef helping me into the back of a car. It wasn't The Frog, so it must have been a taxi. She got in beside me and told the driver to take us to Psych Emergency.

CHAPTER EIGHT

What chance has a person with bipolar disorder and/or Asperger's Syndrome of becoming an author? What chance have I of publishing my diary, or of writing a bestseller, when sometimes I cannot even understand or rein in my own emotions?

It turns out that I'm in good company.

Famous authors who had bipolar disorder:
Agatha Christie, Ernest Hemingway, Graham Greene, Edgar Allan Poe, Virginia Woolf

Famous authors who have Autism or Asperger's Syndrome, or, in their case, perhaps it should be awe-tism:
Dr Temple Grandin ("Thinking In Pictures")
Rudy Simone ("Aspergirls")
Liane Holliday Willey ("Pretending To Be Normal")
John Elder Robison ("Look Me In The Eye")

Clever characters from fiction speculated to have Autism or Asperger's Syndrome:
Sherlock Holmes
Lisbeth Salander (The Girl with the Dragon Tattoo)

I was in the hospital for several days. There were lots of people to talk to and to take care of me. Doctors with their writing pads, nurses with their laptops, all asking me questions and making notes about me. Everyone there took a great deal of interest in me, watched me carefully, listened intently to everything I had to say and wrote it down. Slowly and gently, they helped me back down to earth from wherever I'd gone in my head. Ever so cautiously, a step at a time, they assisted me to return to my level of normal.

Though it was probably the meds that truly did it. They reintroduced those straight away. After a few days of taking them again, I realised just how far I'd put myself in the way of harm by not getting an urgent prescription for my bipolar meds immediately following the earthquake. And my contraceptive pills. I hadn't replaced them either, and I'd had unprotected sex with Robert and—I cringed—with Angelo while hypomanic and didn't give any thought to the possible consequences. That was frightening.

In my defence, I'd lost my cousin and my home, and my sense of security had been shaken and shattered and ruined as much as part of the city itself.

Fortunately, I'd managed to keep my promise to visit my mother because she was in another part of the hospital. One of the nurses escorted me over there to see her one morning.

When I had been a little girl, people remarked on how well I resembled my mother, but now she bore almost no resemblance to me or to the person she was then. She had deteriorated even in the three months since I'd last seen her and, although only in her mid-fifties, she now looked haggard. Anxiety lines creased her brow, and the shape of her mouth had set in a permanent scowl. She was sitting in the communal lounge when I found her, reading a magazine in the sunlight coming through an open window. There were three other people in the lounge, doing puzzles or reading, and it was quiet.

"How are you, Mum? Were you upset by the earthquake?" I asked, drawing up a chair and sitting down next to her. What a stupid question, I reprimanded myself—of course the earthquake upset her. It stressed everyone out. "Sorry I haven't come in earlier. I—um—have had my own problems. I've been in here a few days myself."

She stared at me and her face twisted into a broken smile for a moment, before resuming its glower. "Chloe. Where have you been, misbegotten daughter? Have you talked to your father recently? Is he here? I don't want to see him if he is. He's cruel. Keep away from me. I know you've been taking things, stealing from me. Stealing! You keep your filthy hands to yourself."

I sat back, overwhelmed. This obviously wasn't a good day for my mother. I knew from experience that soon she would become abusive or distressed. I always seemed to have that effect on her, but it also happens at other random times. Most of what she said wasn't true or simply didn't make any sense. My father was not cruel, for instance; absent, yes, but not cruel.

"I've been manic again, Mum."

"Good, good, good for you." She clearly wasn't listening, and she was looking out of the window at something. "You're a clever girl, Chloe, I always said you were. Too clever. But always taking my things, always spying on me. Are you still at university?"

At last, a rational question, but not one that I actually wanted to answer. "No. I've missed most of the term so far because I got stressed and depressed and OCD after the earthquake. I don't spy on you, Mum, and I don't steal things. How are you? Are you feeling any better? Are you happy?"

My mother harrumphed. "They feed me spiders in here."

"What was that, Mum?"

"No one comes to visit me. Chloe never comes to visit me."

"Mum! I'm Chloe! I'm here now."

She turned and stared at me. "You can't be. Chloe never visits me."

I left her shortly after that, thinking that my visit had been a waste of time.

Stef came to the hospital to pick me up in the late afternoon the next day. I'd lost track of time, so I wasn't even sure what day of the week it was. I thought Robert might have come to see me during my hospitalisation, but he stayed away the entire time.

Stef called a taxi for us, and we sat on the grass outside the main entrance, waiting for it to arrive. It was warm, and I wore a sleeveless top (a green one, because it was a Thursday, and I had managed to replace some of my clothes since the earthquake). I also wore my beret because I felt anxious after my time in the hospital, wondering if I was ready to face the world again.

"Have you heard from Ingrid? Any news of Marinda?"

"My mother's beside herself," said Stef, and I was momentarily puzzled by the odd expression as I tried to visualise it. "She fears the worst. I'm not ready to accept that, yet."

"We'll find out sometime what happened." Obviously. What a stupid thing to say, I chided myself, but, really, what was there to say? We are just waiting for answers.

"I guess that's inevitable. A dedicated police officer talks to her every day, and someone came around yesterday to take DNA samples from Marinda's hairbrush."

"Do you think you'll ever get The Frog back?" I asked after a few moments of contemplation.

"I think so, Chloe. Apparently, the military will bring all the cars out when it's deemed safe. Maybe in another couple of weeks or so. But it's in the Red Zone. I can't even get near the car park building myself. I have to wait for the army to get it out."

"I suppose you don't even know what condition it's in, do you? Like whether it's drivable or just a mash of mangled steel and rubber."

"No." She sighed. "At least I'm getting fit by walking to work every day."

"Yeah. And how is work now?"

"We've relocated to an old warehouse in Phillipstown, as there's so little proper office space available. It's stinking hot in there, even with the portable air conditioners they've brought in. And I've had to start a lot of my projects again. I don't have any of my folders. We were allowed back into the old building, accompanied by engineers, for five minutes only to collect vital business records, but I didn't want to go in." Stef shuddered.

"Yeah. Fair enough." I was silent for a while, thinking. "Thanks, Stef. For bringing me here. I sort of lost control for a while."

"You think?"

"Why didn't Robert come? He hasn't visited me in

here. He didn't even call. Can you believe it? Is he busy at uni or something? I've really missed having time with him." I hesitated as a horrible thought occurred to me. "Nothing's happened to him, has it?"

"Um..."

"Um, what? What's going on, Stef?"

"Look, here's the taxi now."

A large sedan taxi pulled up next to us, and the young, well-muscled Samoan driver jumped out. "Hey, yous the ones for a ride to Linwood?"

"That's us," said Stef, getting to her feet. I followed, lifting my carry-bag. All it had was a few changes of clothes and a few books, but it was heavy. Probably because of the books. The medical staff had advised me not to have my laptop with me in my psychological state. They'd told me to leave anything with internet access at home.

"Sweet as," grinned the huge man. He grabbed my over-stuffed bag and put it in the car boot as if it were as light as one of the new iPads. We all got into the car, Stef and I getting into the back seat together.

The driver started the car and swung it around in a U-turn on the quiet road. "I'm Kaperielu. Would yous like some music?"

"Yes, thanks," said Stef.

Kaperielu switched on the radio, and easy-listening music streamed out of it quietly. "Yous are lucky music is free in my taxi." He glanced up at the rear-view mirror, which he tilted so he could see us. "In Finland, the taxi drivers there has to pay royalties for playing music in theirs cabs. Okay, I'm going to take yous a longer way today. I has to detour to the south of the city because the traffic is very bad and many roads are blocked off."

He hit the accelerator.

"What's going on with Robert?" I asked Stef again.

"Um... well..."

"Just tell me. I don't want to have to guess."

"Aah... perhaps he should tell you himself."

"Why? What is it?"

"That's just it. It would be better coming from him. God, I didn't want to talk about this now. We haven't even got you home yet."

"We're not talking about it. We're talking about not talking about it. I'm trying to talk about it, but you haven't said anything. What's going on, Stef?"

She stayed silent, not even looking at me. I waited fourteen seconds, an incredible feat of patience for me, and then asked again, "What is it you're not telling me?"

"I can't tell you. Sorry. You need to talk to Robert."

I took a deep breath and let out a loud sigh. This was intensely frustrating. Stef appeared unwilling to answer me, and I didn't know why. She must have known her reticence would upset me, but either didn't care or, perhaps, did not want to share the truth, whatever it was. Robert wasn't dead, obviously, for Stef had told me to talk to him directly, but almost any other scenario might be possible. A multitude of possibilities, some of them dire or bizarre, presented themselves in my mind. The stress and uncertainty made me shudder. This wasn't what I needed on my way home from the psychiatric hospital.

Kaperielu spoke gently. "Boyfriend trouble?"

"I don't know," I groaned.

True to his word, Kaperielu took us through some of the southern suburbs, bypassing the cordoned-off central city and the surrounding main roads, which were apparently choked with traffic. Though the quake had damaged many vehicles or rendered them unreachable, there seemed to be more cars on the road than ever. Maybe it was because many of the roads were damaged, torn, cracked or potholed and weren't safe for bicycles, so more people took to their cars. Or perhaps it was because the roads were in such a state that getting anywhere took longer, adding to the traffic because everyone had to slow down.

Everyone except Kaperielu, evidently. His taxi was an upmarket vehicle with suspension that was currently good, but probably wouldn't be for much longer. We lurched from side to side in the back seat whenever he swerved around potholes, and we bounced up and down whenever he hit one or drove over the bumps and dips in the road surface caused by the earthquake. There were a lot of those.

Sometimes, he gestured out of the window and made a passing comment or two: "I saw a car in a sinkhole there. And there—see that rubble?—there wuz a dairy and a fish 'n' chip shop there, and they both collapsed."

Stef said no more to me on the way home, even though I asked her three more times what it was that she wasn't telling me about Robert. Rigid thinking and rumination are core parts of my Aspie nature. Thinking of all the possible explanations was exhausting and upsetting for me. Stef knew that, though, but still she didn't tell me. Maybe she was trying to make me feel bad, but I didn't know why.

A few minutes later, we were back at Marinda's house. Kaperielu retrieved my bag and handed it to me with a smile. Stef paid him the fare, and he waved goodbye to us.

Despite my burning desire to speak to Robert, I'd worked myself up to a state of anxiety about two notches short of a full-blown panic attack. I would have asked Kaperielu to take me back to the hospital had it not been for my need to know what Stef wasn't telling me. Was Robert hurt? Sick? That would explain why he hadn't visited or called me. Was he angry at me? Or was it something else I hadn't thought of?

"Let's go in," said Stef. She gave me a weak smile rather than her usual shining *gleamer*. "I'll make you some green tea."

I found Robert upstairs, lying on his bed, reading a book titled *Panic*. It was probably some kind of contemporary economics book rather than an Armageddon novel, though there does seem to be a lot of overlap between them nowadays. I hoped the title wasn't auspicious for our reunion. At least Robert didn't appear to be sick or injured.

"Hi," I said from the doorway.

"Hi." Robert sat up. He put a *Hobbit* bookmark inside his book and placed it on the bedside table.

"I'm feeling much better now," I said. I assumed he was going to ask me the question.

"That's good." Something on the carpet held Robert's complete attention.

"I was a bit out of control for a while. You didn't notice, though, did you?"

"Sorry, Chloe, I thought it was just earthquake stress." Now the opposite wall attracted his steely gaze.

I went over to his bed, sat down and turned to face him. I wasn't sure, but it seemed that he swayed away a little. In any case, he didn't reach over to give me a cuddle, but I couldn't infer anything from that. He might just want non-physical time at the moment.

"Why didn't you come and visit me, or call? I didn't know what was going on with you. I tried to get Stef to tell me on the way home, but she didn't. I've been worried about you, which is ridiculous really, seeing as I was the one admitted to the psychiatric hospital. But I expected to see you, or at least to hear from you. What's happened? Have you been really busy at uni?"

Robert looked directly at me but said nothing. I waited, unable to discern the expression on his face, if indeed he even had one that Non-Spectrum people would be able to interpret. After a few moments, I realised that I'd asked him too many questions at once, and he was probably struggling with what to say.

"Just tell me why you didn't come to see me," I said. "We'll talk about it."

"I was on my way to visit you," he started, "the day you were admitted. When I got home from university that day, Stef told me that she'd taken you in, that apparently you weren't taking your meds—"

"I'd lost them in the earthquake!"

"I know, but you didn't get them replaced, did you? You were acting strangely. Stef and I were worried about you. She told you to see your doctor and get back on your meds, yet you didn't."

"Are you accusing me of something?" I couldn't hear any tone of accusation in his voice. It may or may not have been there. But the words themselves indicated accusation.

"Yes."

Typical Aspie answer, I thought. "Why didn't you come to visit me?" I asked yet again. "You said you were on your way. What happened?"

"I went to get a takeaway coffee at Café Gorgon."

I'm sure my heart stopped beating for a few moments. I could guess what Robert was going to say. I hadn't forgotten what happened, though I'd tried.

"I was about to go in, then I noticed that Italian barista standing outside, smoking a cigarette. He had such a big grin on his face that I asked him what he was so happy about. He bragged that he'd been down for a shower earlier that afternoon and had sex, he said, 'with a hot chick with a blue patch of hair'."

"Um..."

"In fact, he described you quite clearly when I asked him about it further. It's true, isn't it, Chloe? You had sex with him in the showers, didn't you?"

I sighed. "Yes, it's true, but a bipolar manic episode caused me to act uncharacteristically at the time, remember."

"Does that make any difference?"

"Of course it does. I wasn't in my right mind. I didn't think about the consequences of my actions. Hell, I wasn't even thinking at all!"

"That was obvious."

"It wasn't really my fault, Robert."

"You knew what you were doing, though. You could have turned around and walked away from the situation."

"I never actually even thought of that. I'm sorry. I can't do anything about it now. It was a crazy time. I wasn't acting normally. It wasn't really me. Well, I know it was me, but it was the 'me' without my meds, as high as a kite. Not the 'me' on the meds who doesn't do crazy stuff like that. Do you understand?"

"No."

Another typically terse Aspie answer, I noted. "Will you

at least try to forget about it?"

"No. Not yet." Robert slid off the bed and paced—almost stomped—to the door, where he spun around to face me. "I feel hurt, Chloe. I need you to leave me alone for a while."

"Sure. How long?"

"I don't know. A few days, maybe a few weeks. But we're breaking up."

"Are we?" I said, but Robert had turned around and left the room.

Now I got off the bed, racing after him before he could disappear down the stairs. I caught him half-way along the hall. "I can't believe you're breaking up with me over one little misadventure while I was having a manic episode."

"Yeah? Well, I am."

I couldn't help but think Robert's words were immature and that he was acting like a peeved school kid. But maybe he would reconsider after we had some time apart. I hoped so. I felt awful at what he'd said. My stomach churned, and I felt a headache coming on at warp speed.

"Will you at least think about it for a while and reconsider later? It didn't mean anything. I was a bit out of control, like I told you before. It's not actually my fault. It was just a bad five minutes."

Robert stared directly at the wall next to us. "Is that how long it took? Never mind. Don't answer that. We're breaking up, Chloe. At least for now." He started to move away, towards the stairs. I reached out and grabbed his arm before he could get away.

"Wait, Robert. There are things we've got to talk about."

We had power again, which I discovered by noticing that the light in my room was on. I'd left the switch on so I could see when the power was restored. Putting my conversation with Robert out of my mind for the moment, I stood on a chair and disconnected my laptop from the solar battery so I could reconnect it to mains power.

When I got down, cable in hand, I noticed Stef standing in the doorway.

"Hi. Wanna talk?" she asked.

I threw the cable onto the floor under the window. "Now you want to talk. Why didn't you tell me in the taxi that Robert was going to break up with me? You knew, didn't you?"

Stef came into the room and sat on the edge of the bed. "Yes, I did. He'd told me. But, like I said to you, it was better that he tell you himself in person at home than I do it in the taxi."

"No, it wasn't. I was upset. I was worried that something had happened to him. You should have just told me."

She was silent for a few moments, gazing at me with an expression I couldn't decipher. Finally, she said, "How do you feel, Chloe? Are you okay? Do you want to talk about it, or are you too shell-shocked?"

"Shell-shocked?"

"I mean, are you too stunned to be able to think clearly?"

"No, I'm okay." I surprised myself by saying this, as I realised it was true. At least partially.

"Really?"

I nodded. "I'm sad, but I'm all right."

"So... do you want me to ask Robert to move out? Have

you discussed it with him?"

"No, of course not. Why do you think I would want you to ask Robert to move out?"

"Isn't it going to be uncomfortable for you living in the same house as Robert now?"

"No, why would it be?"

"Well... obviously... because you were a couple and now you're not? Whenever that happens, usually one person moves out. And I'm not going to make you move out, Chloe, you're my cousin. So it would have to be Robert."

"No, he doesn't have to move out. We still have our separate rooms. That's fine. It's a good arrangement."

"But won't you feel uncomfortable with Robert when you're eating with him? Watching TV with him? Won't having him around remind you of you two being a couple?"

Stef's tenacity on this point irritated me. I realised she was probably only trying to help me, to protect me from something she imagined would be hurtful. I honestly didn't know. Nor did I think she understood either.

"Yes, probably, but that's a good thing," I said, raising my voice a few decibels. "We liked being a couple, so why wouldn't I want to be reminded of it? And remember, we lived as flatmates for months before we started sleeping together. We're just going back to that, really. That wasn't uncomfortable at all. I like having him around. We've *decoupled*, but we haven't *defriended*."

"Chloe, I'm just trying to help—"

"I know. But, really, it's no problem. I made a mistake when I was off my meds, and Robert is upset by it. Hell, why wouldn't he be? And, because of that, he's decided we can't be a couple anymore. I have to live with that for now. But he's still my friend. I don't want you to send him away. Do you understand that? The fact that he no longer wants to be my boyfriend is more than enough change for me to deal with at the moment. If you force him to leave, then we'll have to find another flatmate, probably someone we don't know, and—" I choked on the words and stopped abruptly. I wasn't even sure what I was going to say. The words had just been flooding out.

Stef stared at me in an unusual way. Maybe intently, or with curiosity as to what I might say next. But I wasn't going to say anything next. I couldn't think of anything more to say.

"All right, Chloe," she said slowly, "I won't make Robert leave."

She turned to go, then paused and glanced back at me over her shoulder. "We'll talk later, if you want to, okay?"

I listened to her walk downstairs. When her footfalls on the carpeted stairs had faded to nothing, I got up and closed the door quietly. I went over to a spot under the window in my room that I liked because, at this time of the day, the sun streams in, and it warms a small area, and sometimes I feel comfortable sitting in the sunlight there. I sat cross-legged and started rocking, gnawing my knuckles, as silent tears began to flow.

CHAPTER **N**INE

I'm good at finding part-time jobs, probably because I've had so much practice at it. What I'm not good at, though, is keeping them. Of course, there are plenty of jobs I've applied for and not got, but there are none for which I haven't been hired and fired in quick succession.

Before my collection of alphabet disorders diagnosi, I was emotionally a wreck. I'd get hired because I could prove to my employers I was hard-working, enthusiastic and organised. The following month, they'd swear I was a different person, constantly irritable, always late and unmotivated. I'd realise everything was going wrong—again—and end up in hospital for a spell. Inevitably, I no longer had a job when I came out.

After I became accustomed to the psychiatrist's couch, my juggling act of work and medical appointments began. Often, I couldn't get time off to attend my appointments, so I either didn't go and my treatment suffered, or I went anyway, absent without leave, and got fired the next day upon my return to work. My bipolar diagnosis was swiftly followed by a series of ever-changing medications as the doctors experimented, like medieval alchemists, to find out what might work for me. A myriad of side effects accompanied these. I'd puke in the toilets at work because of the meds. Fall asleep at work because of the meds. Or I'd be clumsy, or snappy, but mostly I'd be zombified. I'd stare blankly at my colleagues and the world, sometimes unable to think, reason or respond, as if I were a member of the walking undead. They thought I was taking a lot of illegal drugs, but I wasn't—I took only the pharmaceuticals prescribed for me. Yet sometimes the side effects would be so severe that I'd go off the meds, have another relapse, and get fired again from whatever part-time job I'd managed to wheedle my way into. I was always too afraid and too ashamed to tell my co-workers what was going on with me.

I avoided Robert and Stef the next morning, waiting in my room until I was sure they had both gone out, Stef to work, Robert to university. They walked out of the house together at 8.26 a.m. Stef had got into the habit of walking to work because she still did not have her car back, and Robert walked to the bus stop to catch the Orbiter.

I lay on my bed for a long while, staring at the wall and stimming by bending my right arm at the elbow and letting it fall back onto the duvet in a slow, rhythmic pattern. It made a slow, gentle 'doff' each time, kind of like the dulled tock-tick of a muffled clock on sedatives. It was soothing and focussing at the same time. I felt myself entering a trance-like state and stayed there for some time, trying to remember all that had happened to me over the past few days and weeks, process it, separate out what was my fault and what had been out of my control, what was due to Mother Nature and what happened because I'd gone off my meds. After twenty-two minutes, I felt calmer, even though I hadn't managed to answer some of my own questions. Just thinking through the issues seemed to bring some relief. I got up and dressed.

It was a cloudy, early autumn day. I still couldn't face even the thought of returning to uni, let alone go back to lectures and handing in assignments, so I decided to go for a walk. I thought that might also help me clear my head a little.

We still had no running water, so I poured myself a glass of water from our water tanker supplies. That was more convenient anyway, at least for drinking; most of the city had running water by now, but it had to be boiled and cooled before drinking. The sewer damage throughout the city meant that our once pure water wasn't yet free from contamination.

After a few moments, I remembered that we had power in the house, and I made myself some toast and a coffee. A strong one. It was odd, I thought, how I'd switched from green tea to coffee, but I couldn't imagine going back. There was something about drinking a lot of coffee that helped me cope with my life. My absurdly turned-upside-down life, in which I now felt a virtual stranger.

I had my breakfast in silence. Usually, I spent this time with Robert, either talking or just quietly spending time together in that easy, undemanding ambiance of soulmates. Our time together over breakfast used to generate a feeling of warmth and well-being in me. Today, eating breakfast by myself was a stark contrast; like my toast, cold, soggy and unfulfilling.

I was certainly ready for my walk after that, and I left the house, congratulating myself on having remembered to lock it and to take my bag with me this time. That was a definite improvement. Perhaps my mind had settled down a little, returning to whatever crazy lopsided level might be considered 'normal' for me. My head still felt like a racetrack, though, around which random thoughts and ruminations careered wildly.

I walked for quite some time, keeping away from other pedestrians whenever possible because I didn't feel like exchanging the little fake social niceties that people like to do when meeting strangers or even people they know only by sight. A 'hello' or 'g'day' might be expected to evolve into an on-the-spot unplanned conversation that I'm really no good at and have no interest in because it's so inconsequential. It irritates me that people who serve me in a shop might ask how I am, and ask everyone the same questions, even though they couldn't possibly care how all their customers are unless they are collecting data for the secret service or some national survey or something. Even worse is when they ask what plans I have for the day. What business is it of theirs? And I usually haven't even decided on my plans anyway.

My old house came into view before I even realised I'd walked that way. I stopped, stunned, wondering for a minute if I were dreaming and sleepwalking. I'd been following the river for a while, and I was now at the tree in which Robert and I had unsuccessfully tried to make love on the evening that I returned to Christchurch from Australia. That seemed so long ago now, a lifetime or more, as so much had happened in the intervening time—the earthquake, Marinda's disappearance, the loss of my cat Sex, the loss of the house we were living in at the time forcing us to move, my dropping out of university, my manic episode, my financial and sexual misadventures, my hospitalisation, the sad breaking up with Robert.

Yeah, life sucked.

I stood under the tree, looking across the road at the abandoned house, just one of many such ruins in the desolate eastern suburbs. Even more of the roof appeared to have collapsed inwards into the upstairs bedrooms, probably as a result of the frequent aftershocks. Tall metal netting fences had been erected all around it, hooked together and sealed at the driveway by a large padlock. One of the familiar red stickers denoted that it was uninhabitable, and other signs warned of 'Danger!' and advised 'No Entry'.

I stood there for what felt like ages, studying the contours of the ruined building and listening to the quiet sounds of the slowly running river. At one point, there was a low rumbling, followed by a gentle rolling motion, announcing another aftershock. Probably a 'three point four' or a 'three point five' out west.

The brisk breeze brushed the hair around my face and rustled the leaves on the branches above me as I stared obsessively at the house, unable even to determine how I felt about it. I didn't think I felt angry, or upset, or afraid, or regretful, or guilty, or any of the other feelings that I sometimes couldn't completely identify within myself. I couldn't even work out why I cared. After all, I'd only lived there for a few days. I had no ties to it, apart from the fact that almost all of my possessions were inside. But, I guess, this broken house had come to symbolize the whole dysfunction of the earthquake situation in a single physical form that I could relate to.

Perhaps fate had led me to take this route today back to the old wrecked house. I decided that my journey would not be wasted. Though I knew Robert had been looking for our lost cat, Sex, almost every day without success, I would take a last look too. I'd realised long ago that she had probably perished in the house, or run away out of fear and got lost. She could be anywhere. And, if I couldn't find her, I would see if there was anything I could retrieve from the house itself. Though it would be unlikely, as rainwater must have further damaged the contents.

I sensed that someone was behind and beside me, and spun around. A tall, lanky man stood a few metres away, puffing on a roll-up cigarette and watching me. I recognised my old neighbour, the one with the loud car and the turbulent teenagers.

"Where's your boyfriend?" he asked, nodding slightly at the tree. I remembered him pulling me out of the water that night.

"We broke up."

He took another drag and turned slightly away from me to look across the road at his own wrecked house. "Sorry to hear that."

I followed his gaze. His house wasn't damaged to nearly the extent of the house I'd been living in, but I could see a large crack in the brickwork running most of the way up the front exterior. The chimney had fallen off. My neighbour's noisy car stood forever silent now, buried under a pile of bricks from the fallen chimney.

"Red-stickered," said the man needlessly. "Like yours. I come back and look at it every day, just wondering why Avonside was hit so hard. We lost our homes, the roads here are ripped up, there was liquifaction all over the place, and nearly everyone in the street has abandoned their properties to move elsewhere. I don't see people around here now except for sightseers, looters and taggers. Yet in the north and west of the city, nearly everything's normal. You'd hardly know there'd been an earthquake."

"The university was damaged, and there are shops and churches down in Papanui," I said.

"Yeah, but most people didn't lose their homes over that side of town, did they?" he snapped.

"No, that's true."

"I just don't understand why. Why here? Why us? What's the reason behind it all?"

"It's just random," I said. "There's no 'why'. It just is

that way. We couldn't have known about it beforehand, and we couldn't have done anything about it anyway if we had. It's bad luck for us, but it's just random."

The man faced me before continuing. I had the impression that if I hadn't been there, he probably would have complained to the tree instead. "I had to take my family to a shelter for a week until I could find somewhere else for us to live. I came back here and got a few things out of the house and the garage before they red-stickered it, but not much. Now, I just come back to look at the place, trying to understand why it happened."

"No reason. It was just random," I repeated. I didn't know why he couldn't understand this.

"And why are you here? Just looking at your house too? You were renting, weren't you? And you'd only just moved in, so why would you be attached to the place? It's nothing to you. Why are you here?"

"I'm looking for Sex." Shit, I thought. He might misconstrue that.

The gangly man took one last drag on his cigarette and flicked it into the river. "Well, I can help you out with that, at least. But not in the tree, please."

I knew he'd misunderstand me. "No, that's not what I meant. I have—"

"Relax. I'm just kiddin' ya. I know you meant your lost cat. I've talked to your ex-boyfriend plenty of times about it. He never found any trace of her."

"I know. But I'm going to look one last time. And," I added, glancing at him, "see if there's anything salvageable left in the house, if I can get into it."

"Didn't you get out what you could before it got red-stickered?"

"No." I didn't want to explain the reasons why I hadn't, not because I had no wish to share that with him, but simply because I did not want to go over it all again in my own mind.

I bade my gangly ex-neighbour goodbye. I still didn't even know his name, but I didn't see the point in asking either. We weren't neighbours anymore, and I probably wouldn't see him again. This put our relationship on the bottom rung of the ladder of social intercourse, one that I wouldn't waste time or expend energy on.

I climbed another large tree—oak, I think—standing outside the fence to our old rented house. A large bough extended outwards over the metal fence. I hoped the limb was weight-bearing and cautiously edged along it. The rough bark was uncomfortable on my bum. Soon, though, I'd passed above the metal fence. I carefully lowered myself from the thick bough and dropped the last thirty centimetres to the ground.

The house appeared even eerier and gloomier now that I was closer to it. A glance at what was left of the roof told me that I couldn't expect to find anything upstairs that hadn't escaped the rain we'd had since the earthquake, as the hole up there had expanded. I walked over to the broken kitchen window and looked inside. A foul smell assailed me from within, and I dry-retched.

There was plenty of sunlight streaming in. The kitchen hadn't been touched since the earthquake. Inside, I could see the refrigerator lying on one side, its doors open, most of the contents spilled out and mixed up on the floor into some kind of lumpy pool of stinking, rotting multi-coloured hash that was most certainly all past its use-by date. Some creatures had attacked the plastic containers that had survived the earthquake and left gnaw marks on them—probably rodents.

I turned away. I would not be able to salvage anything from there. Not without risking some horrible disease, anyway.

I walked a little further along the front of the house and peered through one of the living room windows. It was in partial shadow, and I couldn't make out everything in the room at first. I had to wait for my eyes to adjust to the lower level of light in the room. There was something odd about the stairs. They looked out of place. After a minute or so, once my eyes had adjusted to the gloom, I could see why they looked out of place. It was because they were no longer attached to the top floor and they'd yawed sideways into the living room a metre or two. Belatedly, I remembered Robert telling me this when we came back to the house on the day of the earthquake. A few loose bricks from the collapsed chimney adorned some of the upper steps. Below, in the living room itself, was a pool of rainwater that had come in through the cavity left by the chimney and cascaded off the landing.

"You shouldn't be in here."

The voice startled me, and I jumped. It was my old neighbour again. He must have followed me.

"I know," I said. "I don't even know why I'm here. I just went out for a walk by myself and came here without ever intending to. Maybe, subconsciously, I wanted to see the place again. Even though I only lived here a few days, it's where all my stuff is. Then I thought that, maybe, I could rescue some of my stuff, but I can't. Everything's wet and mouldy and chewed by rodents and spoiled. It looks too dangerous to go inside anyway, and there's no way I can get upstairs even if I wanted to take the risk."

My neighbour sighed, expelling smoke from a new roll-up cigarette. "I know. Your place is a wreck. Mine wasn't so badly hit. I managed to get some of my stuff out the next day, some clothes and photos and personal crap, but I couldn't move any of the big furniture out. It wasn't safe. They red-stickered it not long after that. You do know you're not allowed in here, don't you?"

"I know," I said, then paused. I had a sense of déjà vu and didn't want to repeat myself further. "Thanks, anyway. I'm just going to look around for my cat and then I'll go."

"Sure. Sure." He took out another cigarette and lit it slowly. "I'll watch out for you. I saw some teenagers hanging around earlier, probably up to trouble. I'll wait here for you in case they come back."

"That's kind of you. Thanks." Maybe my ex-neighbour wasn't a bad sort after all, but more of a rough diamond kind of character. I started walking around the perimeter of the house, looking under any plants or shrubs large enough to hide Sex, but there was no sign of her. Around the back of the house, I paused longer by the back porch. The porch frame was badly warped, the door slightly ajar. I peered through the crack, wondering if Sex had crawled in there and curled up to sleep. She wasn't there, but I could see her food bowl, empty and forgotten. I looked grimly at it, wondering if she had run away and another family had adopted her.

I was about to turn away and carry on the search when I spotted my rollerblades just inside the door. I had always left them there, and there they still were. The gap between the door and the frame looked too small for them, though. I could reach them, but I wouldn't be able to get them out unless I opened the door further. Would it be safe to do that? I wondered. Or would it bring the whole building down like a house of cards? I didn't know, but I decided to find out. With both hands, I pulled the door gently towards me a few centimetres until it got stuck. The house remained standing, and nothing untoward happened. Grinning, I slipped my hand in and pulled out my rollerblades. Got them! I'd rescued something from the house after all!

I got to my feet happily, walked around the next corner, and suddenly came upon a tall kid with a spray can, busy tagging the width of the house with blue paint. He jumped back when he saw me, clearly surprised at the interruption to his act of vandalism. He looked about fifteen or sixteen.

"Hey!" I shouted at him. "What do you think you're doing?"

He didn't answer but rushed straight at me. Before I could move, he barged into my shoulder and knocked me sideways into the wall of the house. Momentarily, I feared that I might bring the whole thing toppling down onto me, but it didn't happen, and I slid down to the ground. Dazed, I spun around, shouting "Stop!"

The youth did stop at the corner of the house, pausing to turn in my direction. The shadow from his hooded sweater concealed most of his face, and I couldn't make out his features or expression. I didn't know if he'd stopped to see if I'd been hurt, or to see if I was coming after him, or what. But I still felt a little stunned by my collision with the brick wall of the house, and I couldn't even get to my feet at the moment.

Suddenly, he dashed towards me, and I screamed as I thought he was going to kick me, but he didn't. He scooped up my rollerblades in his free hand, took off again and raced around the corner of the house.

I scrambled to my feet, intending to give chase as best as I could. Having rescued my rollerblades from the ruined house, I didn't want to lose them straight away to some young thieving vandal.

I went after him, even though I knew he was too fast for me. I rounded the side of the house and saw my ex-neighbour and the youth tussling together. I guessed he'd heard my scream and wanted to stop the teenager from getting away until he knew if I was all right. Also, he'd have been able to see the kid was a tagger as he still had his spray paint can in his right hand.

My ex-neighbour won the tussle and sat on the youth, pinning him to the ground. "He was tagging the house. And those are my rollerblades he tried to steal," I growled as I approached. The rollerblades lay on the ground close by. I picked them up thoughtfully.

"Is that so?" asked my ex-neighbour. "And did you work your graffiti on the house next door too? My house?"

The tagger responded with an inventive string of expletive combinations, some of which I'd never heard before and hopefully never would again.

"I think that's a 'yes'," I deduced.

"Right, then. Pass me that spray can, will you?"

I picked up the paint sprayer, passed it to my ex-neighbour and looked on with interest.

We let him go a couple of minutes later, but in that time, we accomplished quite a bit of artwork ourselves. We sprayed blue the youth's top-of-the-range white trainers, along with his hooded top and most of his hair. He scampered off without looking back.

My ex-neighbour and I chatted for a few minutes before he said he needed to get back to his wife and kids. After he had departed, I had another look around for Sex, peering amongst shrubs and up into trees, but there was no sign of the little cat. Sad and despondent, I wondered what might have happened to her, whether she'd died in the earthquake or had simply gone away and been adopted by another family. I hoped it was the latter and that she was all right.

I left the same way I'd entered, by clambering along the tree limb over the fence, then dropping to the ground on the other side. The brief haziness I'd had after being knocked into the wall by the tagger had passed and been replaced by a headache. The side of my face felt tender, and I thought it might come up in a bruise later on. I decided to skate home and sat down to put on my rollerblades.

I stood up when I heard shouts and turned to face the direction from which they had come. A group of teenagers advanced towards me, spearheaded by the newly blue boy, who pointed at me and shouted a mixture of threats and obscenities before they all burst into a run.

"Shit," I said.

I snatched up my bag that I'd hidden amongst the exposed tree roots while I investigated the house, then took off as quickly as I could and skated towards the road. The grass and uneven ground made it distressingly slow going. I heard the running footsteps of the group coming closer as I reached the road, but once I got there, I could move faster on the hard surface. A lot faster. Seconds later, I was into full skating stride and racing away from them. I was breathing hard, more from adrenalin than from being out of breath. I skated past several abandoned houses before I dared to risk looking behind me. They had followed, but not far, and had stopped chasing me now, just watching me as I got farther and farther away from them.

I breathed a sigh of relief, but just as I thought I was safe, I skated into a deep crack in the road and went flying forward, landing on my side and scraping my left arm and leg badly. I shouldn't have taken my eyes off the road. There were too many potholes and cracks everywhere after the earthquake.

More shouts came, and they were after me again. I groggily got to my feet, feeling a little dizzy. My arm and leg felt raw and painful. A sharp pain told me that I'd turned my ankle as well. I didn't know if I could outrun them now. I turned, about to skate away again, but I knew I'd be considerably slower.

And I almost ran straight into a taxi. It pulled up right next to me. The passenger window was rolled down, and the driver called out, "Are you all right, miss?"

I didn't answer him. I just jerked the door open, almost fell in, and pulled the door closed behind me.

"Please, get me out of here!"

A familiar voice said, "No problem, miss. I'll get you away."

Kaperielu flashed me a huge Samoan smile, swerved the car around in a tight 180-degree turn, and accelerated.

I was safe.

Kaperielu drove me home. I tried to pay him for the ride, but he wouldn't accept payment. He said that he doesn't charge taxi fares for rescuing people. He even turned down my offer of coming inside for a coffee and cake, saying he had to head off to another job. I watched him drive away, thinking how chivalrous he'd been.

Then I ran to the toilet and vomited. I felt sick after the encounter with the tagger and the fear that he and his friends would catch me. Throwing up actually made me feel a little better. I couldn't take a shower because we still had no running water, and I really wanted one now to wash away the dirt that had accumulated on me from climbing the tree and searching around the old house. I had to make do with dabbing at my scrapes and grazes with antiseptic and bottled water.

Only after that did I pick up the phone and report the incident to the police. After ascertaining that I was safe, the operator told me police officers would come to talk to me later that day. That was fine. I wasn't planning to go anywhere for a while. I needed time to settle myself down.

I made a coffee and drank it while I considered what to do next. My life had turned upside down. I'd dropped out of uni again, and while theoretically I could go back and catch up on my missed lectures, I couldn't face the prospect of studying with all that had happened in my life recently. I needed something else to do, something to work on, or at least to keep me occupied. For a while, I pondered over whether I should try writing a bestseller after all. How hard could it be? It would certainly keep me busy, though I would probably have to cultivate a coffee or alcohol dependency to do it properly, like professional writers.

I decided there was no easy answer to that question. But at least I could keep up my diary, which so far read like a guide on how to go crazy and fuck up your life. I'd lost my boyfriend, dropped out of uni, been hospitalised, moved house twice, lost almost all of my stuff in the earthquake as well as my cat and almost certainly my cousin, gambled away most of my savings, and fallen over while being chased by a group of youths. What could go wrong next? I wondered.

Nothing, I decided after a few minutes' thought. This was the low ebb. Things could only get better from this point. There wasn't much scope in my life for further deterioration.

A loud knocking at the front door interrupted my thoughts. I went to answer it. On the steps stood two police officers with whom I was already familiar, the police sergeant with the bushy eyebrows and a policewoman.

"Chloe Wilson? We're pleased to find you here. I'm glad we remembered where you live."

"Wow. That was quick," I said, wondering why they had to remember my address when I'd given it over the phone less than an hour before. "I'm glad you're here. I want to talk about this. See if you can do something about it. Come in."

They followed me inside to Marinda's living room. Even though we'd been living in it for weeks, I couldn't help but think of the house still as Marinda's, despite her probably being dead, because all of the furniture and pictures and everything else was hers. We'd lost all of our stuff in the earthquake, and we had to put up with the atrocious décor in her house, pink wallpaper and flowery sofas and all. It really felt as if I was living in someone else's home, even though I knew Marinda would probably never return to it.

"That's so good of you to be this cooperative," said the sergeant, taking a seat on one of the flowery sofas. The policewoman sat down next to him and took a notepad and pen out of her pocket.

"Well, of course I'll cooperate fully. It was a crime, after all, and the perpetrator has to be punished for it if possible."

"Excellent," said the sergeant, beaming. "Seldom do we hear such sentiments when making this kind of inquiry. So, you freely admit you were involved, do you?"

I made a face. "Of course I was. But no one saw the incident itself. Is that going to be a problem? I mean, gathering evidence and all?"

"Not if you're going to make a full confession."

"Um..." Something sounded wrong with this.

"Why don't you start by telling us why you took the car?"

Shit! I thought. They're not here about that tagger at all! It's about that dairy owner's car I took during my manic episode. He must have given a description of me to the police.

"Um... I can explain that... but first, I thought you were here because of the assault I reported."

"You've been assaulting people as well as stealing their cars?" asked the sergeant. "That wasn't reported to us."

"No! Someone assaulted me! A tagger deliberately knocked me over when I discovered him tagging my old house."

"Your face does look like it's coming up with a bruise. And I see your left arm has a rather bad scrape." The policewoman spoke for the first time. "What happened exactly?"

I turned my attention to her. "I went back to my red-stickered house to see if there was anything I could retrieve from it, but there wasn't, as it's so badly damaged, except for a pair of rollerblades from the porch. I encountered a tagger there spray-painting it. He knocked me into the side of the house as he escaped." I thought it best to omit the details about pinning him down and spraying his hair blue. "Then, he went to get his friends, and they all chased me until I got away."

"This was a red-stickered property, you said?" asked the police sergeant. "How did you get access?"

"I climbed the tree outside to get over the fence." *Admittedly, this didn't sound good.*

"Go on."

"Well, that's it. That's all that happened. Can you do anything about it?"

The policewoman stopped scribbling on her notepad and looked up. "It depends on whether we can find the tagger and link him to the scene. Otherwise it's just your word against his."

"What about this?" I said, pointing to the bruise forming on my head.

"But if no one saw it happen…" She left the rest of the sentence unfinished. I assumed that wasn't promising.

"We will look into it. I'll also arrange for a patrol car to look around the area for the tagger and his mates, in case they're still hanging around," said the sergeant. "Now, about that car…"

I admitted taking the car, and explained the circumstances of my state of mind at the time. I showed them documentation from the hospital and gave them contact phone numbers of the hospital and my doctor. After what seemed an interminable time, but was actually fifty-four minutes, they seemed satisfied with my version of events and got up to leave.

"We'll follow up on this," said the sergeant, "but if it all checks out, I don't think we need to take this matter any further."

I escorted them to the front door. The policewoman turned back to me at the doorway and said, "Take care of yourself, Ms Wilson. Maybe it would be a good idea for you to get some rest."

I watched them go. Rest was something totally alien to me. Probably because I had some kind of undiagnosed hyperactivity disorder or something. I don't know why the whitecoats hadn't diagnosed that when they'd put so many other labels on me. Anyway, I find it hard to relax. I must always be doing something. I'm a person who is driven. The driver is some unknown maniac within me, perhaps, but driven is what I am.

I smiled, and wondered, is that resisting a rest?

CHAPTER TEN

People are different. Not just in how they look, which is obvious, but in how they experience things, which is not evident at all.

If Stef and I go out somewhere together, like to a busy restaurant or for dinner at a friend's house, we are both doing the same thing in the same place at the same time, but our experiences of it are not the same. Each of our experiences is coloured by the unique filter of our individual perception. Stef has an experience filter that is predominantly Non-Spectrum gregarious, but I have an experience filter that is shaded with ASD, bipolar disorder, generalised anxiety disorder, dyscalculia and fuck knows what else.

What stands out to Stef doesn't stand out to me. She loves the buzz of many people talking and can differentiate one voice amongst them from the others. I can't. To me, it is like being at the airport with several jets readying for departure; I can't separate the sound of one from another. She loves bright lights and rotating shiny balls that reflect light beams all over the room. They give me headaches within minutes. She loves the smell and taste of exotic food. I can't eat that; I can only tolerate bland food. With her NS sensitivity and brain processing, she can weave and sway between several conversations with ease in these situations, whereas, for me, everything is too smelly, too bright and far too loud.

The way I see things is like through a kaleidoscope—disjointed and broken, ever-changing, yet somehow beautiful in a structured way. But it makes it hard, sometimes, to identify what people want or even who they are. Especially so with their facial expressions. Their faces don't stay still when they talk, assaulting my senses with a myriad of verbal and visual data.

I have to block out whatever I can; otherwise, I'd be overstimulated within minutes, my brain overwhelmed with the volume of information coming in that it has to interpret and process. That's so exhausting. People think I'm dumb because I don't answer them straight away when they ask me something, but there's a delay between the different parts of my brain, the listening, the thinking and the speaking parts. It's hard to process more than one thing at once, so if I'm trying to listen to someone, I have to block out all visual distractions, for instance.

Social gatherings seem to revitalise NS people. But they make me so weary, just trying to cope with so much going on at once, the masses of sensory input. I guess that, for an NS person, it would be like finding themselves in an electronics shop with all the televisions switched on to different channels at top volume. Yeah, I think it'd be like that for them.

That night, Stef cooked a massive macaroni cheese meal for us, a special one with generous dobs of butter, cut-up strips of bacon and at least three different cheeses, topped with breadcrumbs and crisps. After the day I'd had, all I wanted to do was to stuff myself with comfort food, and this was ideal.

We ate at the table in Marinda's kitchen. I'd stayed

upstairs in my room and only came down when I heard Stef call out that dinner was ready. I'd needed a lot of alone time to digest all of what had happened that day.

"Chloe! You're joining us!" exclaimed Stef as I entered the kitchen. She paused dishing up the meal and rushed over to me. "What happened to your face?"

"I got knocked into the side of our old house by a tagger I discovered there."

Robert swivelled around in his chair. "What were you doing there?"

"I went to look for Sex but, unfortunately, I didn't find any trace of her. While I was there, I came across a tagger defacing the house."

I related the entire event to them both during dinner, swallowing large forkfuls of food whenever one of them interrupted me to ask a question. Stef was the most vocal and inquisitive, remonstrating against taggers, vandals and looters in general. Robert lapsed into a quiet, almost lifeless silence. I think he shut himself down to process it all. Or maybe he was just feeling bad about breaking up with me. I certainly was.

"And the police say they can't do anything?" said Stef, aghast, when I'd finished explaining.

"Probably not, due to lack of evidence, but at least it seems they're not going to charge me with Grand Theft Auto."

"What?"

That sparked another round of questions, all from Stef this time. I told her all about my car theft incident, which seemed hilarious at the time, but was much less so in the cold hard light of rational thought. Robert listened, occasionally shaking his head. I had a second helping of macaroni cheese. The others didn't seem to be eating much, and I didn't like to let it go to waste (though it would probably go to waist, I thought ruefully).

Once I'd finished eating and telling my story, I felt lethargic, weak even, and slightly sick. My head was spinning. I became aware that I was drumming one hand against my thigh and twirling my hair with the other. Unconscious double stimming. I realised that I was suffering from over-anxiety.

Stef noticed. "Are you still seeing your psychotherapist, Chloe? Perhaps you should make an emergency appointment to discuss all this."

That seemed like a good idea, so I did text her and arrange to see her the next day.

I saw her at eleven the next morning. Jacqui was an older woman with a clear head who had supported me tremendously since upper high school. I went over everything that had happened to me with an odd sense of *déjà vu* because I'd already explained it to the police and to my flatmates. It had become tiresome. I still didn't see a solution to my messed-up life. But I guess that is what Jacqui is there for—to help me with that.

"It's as if I'm a trouble magnet," I summed it up. "My life has spun out of control, and I don't know how, or even if, I can repair it. What have I done to deserve this? Whatever it was, it must have been cosmically bad. This is like *Karmageddon*. I don't even know where to begin *desuckifying* my life."

"Well, let's take this one step at a time, Chloe. You've had a hard time lately, and naturally you want to get everything back to normal—to perfect, even—at once. That's not realistic. Getting your medication sorted out was the most important first step. Now, let's evaluate. Do you want to return to uni?"

"No, I don't think so. I've missed too much of the first semester. It'll be far too hard to catch up, and I don't think I'll be able to focus on it anyway. And I feel sick a lot of the time too."

"Yes, well, that's probably due to the stress you're under. You're not the only student to have dropped out of university because of the earthquakes. Some of the foreign students have already flown home. So, how do you think you'll use your time now?"

"Um..."

"That's one thing to consider, then. Now, what about your relationship? How did you feel when your boyfriend broke up with you?"

"Awful, but I can't blame him for that, I guess. He was really upset and felt betrayed by my behaviour when I was manic, I think." These questions were difficult to answer. I didn't know exactly how I should feel about Robert now. I still wanted to spend time with him, and I thought about him touching me, but he'd broken off our relationship. If we were to be together again, he'd have to approach me, and at present, I couldn't imagine that happening. He'd been adamant about it being over.

"Do you think he'll eventually forgive you? Do you want him to? Do you still love him and want to be back together with him?" Jacqui was never short of questions. Her therapy style was challenging and in-your-face. But that was what I needed.

"I love him, yes. I miss the special time we had, just us alone, sharing a meal and doing diabolical Sudoku puzzles, opening up about our feelings or discussing black holes and parallel universes. The way he'd bring the toaster and kettle up to my room and plug them in next to my bed so I could make myself breakfast in bed. He even remembered to bring the bread up, once."

"Does it feel like there's a big hole in your life now without him?"

"Yes." My voice cracked. I dabbed at my eyes with a tissue I pulled from a conveniently-located box next to my chair. "After everything that's happened, I didn't need this..."

"Well, in that case, let's concentrate on keeping you occupied until you get back to a place of normality and serenity for you."

I wish. I don't even know what normality and serenity is.

Jacqui continued. "How about you get a part-time job? That will help you with focus and routine, and get you out of the house for a while. Perhaps you could ask Student Job Search for help with that. Do some exercise, like walking or swimming. Get out and about. Otherwise, occupy yourself with a hobby, something that will give you your own time to yourself and a sense of achievement and belonging. Do you have any ideas?"

"I'm writing a journal."

"Excellent! How cathartic. And is it like a diary of daily events, or a fictionalised memoir?"

"Oh, it's not fiction. It's too strange for that. But I don't know if anyone will ever read it, or even if I would want them to."

"Well, that doesn't matter. It's something you're doing for yourself. We have to make our own music with our lives, even if nobody else sings along. Think about how you can progress with your journal. Any developments in the relationship between you and your mother?"

I told her about the conversation I had with my mother in the psychiatric hospital.

"Hmm, that's difficult. We know she's clearly not in her right mind much of the time, and you had a bad experience that day. But sometimes she is coherent and rational, and you might be able to have some kind of relationship with her then. Now, I'm afraid time's up. That'll be ninety-five dollars, please. Shall I add it to your father's account, as usual?"

"Yes, thanks." The bastard hadn't even come back to Christchurch to see me when I'd been hospitalised. He preferred to be the distant father with a relationship with his chequebook and the postal service instead of with his daughter. Just the same as with my mother, his ex-wife.

"See you next time." Jacqui smiled and got up. That signalled the end of my session. I left, puzzling about what she meant about playing our own music. Was she suggesting I play the violin more? I could do, I suppose.

I decided to take Jacqui's advice literally and be active. After a quick lunch at home, I put on my rescued rollerblades, stuffed a notepad and pen into the back pocket of my jeans, grabbed my handbag and set off towards what I call the BCD.

The roads were in an awful condition. Having fallen the previous day, I now paid much more attention to the ground surface directly ahead of me. Everywhere the roads and footpaths were uneven. Large bumps like super-sized molehills of asphalt acne spotted the surface where the liquifaction had pushed them up. Elsewhere, the authorities had coned off sinkholes large enough to trap cars. Potholes were everywhere, as were large, wide cracks dangerous to my rollerblades or to anyone brave enough to ride a bicycle.

The earthquake had torn up the roads mercilessly, so they appeared neglected for decades. Roadworks were all over the place. On my rollerblades, I could often find a way past them, but car drivers would probably encounter diversions when trying to get anywhere for years to come.

I skated around the entire circumference of the Red Zone cordon, stopping at each intersection to take photos with my mobile phone and, sometimes, to talk to the soldiers standing guard duty (I guess that is what they were doing). I asked a couple of them if they would let me into the Red Zone so I could take photos, but they laughed and said that I wasn't allowed in there without a special permit and an engineer escort. It was simply too dangerous. Many of the buildings were unsafe. Sometimes, more debris would tumble during one of the frequent aftershocks, if it was a 'four' or bigger.

With all the time I spent stopping for photos and chats with soldiers, it took me all afternoon to circumnavigate the cordon. By the end of March, some five weeks after the earthquake, it had already been reduced in size as the clean-up operation and demolition continued, but it still took up the majority of the four avenues area.

I took dozens of photos, maybe a couple of hundred or more, from every angle I could view into the Red Zone. The devastation was unreal, and I knew there was a lot more that I couldn't see from the edge of the cordon. The cathedral, for instance. I could only get a far-off glimpse of the famous spire lying on the ground in front of the ruined structure from two blocks west of Cathedral Square. God, if he exists, had destroyed most of his own houses in Christchurch, including his central icon.

This was the first time I'd seen such devastation. Up to now, I hadn't wanted even to look at it, at the wreckage of my home city, because seeing it only made me want to cry.

Now, I wanted to record it, though of course I would never forget it. The quake had wrecked so many of the towering office blocks, the churches, the retailers on the oldest shopping streets, and all manner of other buildings. At least half of the structures in the CBD would have to be demolished. What I was looking at was the result of the terrifying destructive force of Mother Nature, ripping asunder whatsoever she pleased and changing the lives of everyone in the city forever in a few seconds. I shuddered momentarily, remembering the disturbing dream I'd had.

But it did not look so much like the after effects of any natural event to me. It looked like what was left at the end of a brutal urban civil war, such as pictures I'd seen on TV of the ruins of Beirut or some other far-flung exotic place. Deserted buildings, some with walls or roofs down, others nothing but piles of rubble and vast chunks of decorated stone. All that was missing from this scenario were the bullet holes.

I didn't know what I would do with my photographs, but I wanted to do something. Maybe I could put it all on my blog. *Yes*. That would be the thing to do. A blog, with photos, descriptions, and my personal thoughts on the state of the city. I could upload the *resuburbisation* map that I'd nearly thrown away as well. That would keep me busy. Jacqui would be pleased. She had said keeping occupied with some kind of hobby was what I needed right now.

Of course, writing and maintaining a blog wouldn't bring in any money. I still had to do something about getting a part-time job. And hopefully keeping it for once.

I skated home carefully, pondering various options. It was twilight when I reached our street. I was ready to get home, have a shower and just crash on the sofa. My afternoon's skating and photography of our ruined city had drained me physically, mentally and emotionally, and I felt nauseated again. I'd had the strangest lunch of fried eggs and ice cream, which probably hadn't been a wise choice. Perhaps that was the reason I felt a bit sickly now.

A familiar sight raised my spirits as I swung around the gatepost and into the driveway, and I gave a whoop of joy. Parked in the driveway was The Frog. It appeared dusty but was otherwise in poor condition, which was fine as it's been in poor condition ever since Stef bought it. What I mean is, Stef had got it back undamaged. The authorities had been rescuing and releasing cars from the car park buildings in the Red Zone. Stef was lucky that hers hadn't been damaged at all. That was terrific news.

I rushed inside, ready to congratulate her. I thought she'd be delighted to have her car back, but I found her sitting at the kitchen table, crying. A pile of discarded soggy tissues sat beside an untouched cup of coffee.

"What's wrong?" I blurted out.

Stef looked up at me. "My mother called. She's just spoken to the police. They've identified Marinda's body with the DNA sample. I was prepared for that, of course, but it's still such a shock." She sniffed and seemed about to cry again.

"I'm sorry, Stef."

"Mum said we can stay in the house as long as we want. She'll sort something out with the bank. We can pay rent to her. She's worked it all out. At least we know we've got somewhere to live."

"That's very practical of her," I said. I realised that Ingrid would have planned that a while ago. She'd long given up hope that Marinda would turn up alive, returning from an unannounced holiday or elopement or something. So had I, as I believed what happened in my dream. Stef hadn't ever given up, though, but now she couldn't deny it any longer.

She started weeping again, softly. I went over to her, stood beside her and hugged her. She clung on to me and wouldn't let go for a long time.

CHAPTER **E**LEVEN

Below are things people have said to me about Asperger's Syndrome or Bipolar Disorder. It's as if they forget I'm human too, that I have feelings and thoughts of my own. And these people regard themselves as the 'normal' ones.

"Bipolar? But you don't look crazy."

"You have Asperger's? How awful that must be for you."

"What the hell's wrong with you? Are you retarded or something?"

"Why are you doing that thing with your hands/hair/pen/foot/arm? It looks weird."

"Can't you just not be bipolar/autistic/weird for a while?"

"Hey, do you have any superpowers or anything cool like that, or are you just a geek?"

"You can't have Asperger's. You're not like that guy in The Big Bang Theory."

"Can you fix my computer?"

My mother sat in a comfortable chair in her room and looked out of the window at the park beyond. A book had slipped from her hand and now leaned against the chair on the floor. A mass-market romance novel. No wonder she had fallen asleep.

That was fortunate. I've been meaning to talk to her about something, but I haven't been brave enough to do it. She would probably not understand anyway. She might react by shrieking at me, accusing me of spying on her, of bringing evil spirits with me to harass her or steal her possessions while she sleeps, or blame me for her condition and the sad state of her life. That was always a tough one to hear.

Alternatively, she might not even recognise me, become frightened and tell me to leave her alone. Or she might not care whether I am there to see her or not.

I'd decided that I needed to say all this anyway, even if she doesn't understand or doesn't care. The fact that she was probably sound asleep would actually make it easier. The healing part for me was to be able to tell my mother, not to receive a response from her.

I sat down on the edge of her bed, nearest the chair by the window.

"Mum, I've been thinking about you and Dad and me. I've been thinking a lot about it lately."

I paused there and watched my mother carefully. She didn't move, apart from a gentle rising and falling of her chest, showing that she was still breathing. I had wondered if she were.

"Our family has been split for a long time. I don't even remember when you and Dad were together. I do remember bouncing between your houses week by week, and then spending longer and longer with Dad while you spent more time in here. I remember Dad moving overseas when I was sixteen, and I moved from flat to flat and went waitressing to pay the rent. It was a hard time. But now I think I understand that it was a hard time for you and Dad too. Probably all my life it's been hard for you two."

I rubbed my eyes; they were irritated, possibly by the scent in my mother's room. "It's not my fault. Dad has never blamed me, and although you do, I know that you don't mean it. It's just a symptom of your illness. I know you've suffered a lot from mental illness for many years. I wish you didn't. There's nothing I can do about it, and I hate that. It also scares me. I'm afraid that I'm going to end up like you."

Damned eyes. "There's no love in our family. There must have been once, I guess, when you and Dad met, but all my life, I don't remember him saying he loved you, or you saying you loved him, or either of you saying you loved me. Of course, I didn't care either. I thought that was normal. How would I know any different? And so we all drifted apart, and it was actually better that way. We were all better without each other."

I shifted on the bed, fidgeting with my feet and fiddling with the rings in my ears. I wanted to get up and walk out, but I wasn't finished yet. I watched my mother carefully for any signs of wakefulness, which were not present, and then I continued.

"I hated you both. I really did. You failed me as parents. You failed each other. I've always blamed you and Dad for that, but I've come to realise that it honestly wasn't your fault. You did have good intentions. You did the best you could. It wasn't particularly good, but it was all you could do. I've realised that you made sacrifices for Dad and I, Mum. You were an artist once, and you gave it up. And, in his own way, Dad has made sacrifices too, or thinks he has. He sends money for my psychotherapy. He pays for special treatment and outings for you. Maybe that's all he can do. Maybe he just can't do any more than that. I can see that now. People try their best, and they can only do so much. They're limited because they're human. It's unrealistic to expect more."

I'm rambling. Why does something so clear in my mind always come out so garbled in speech?

"What I'm trying to say, Mum, is that I don't hate you anymore. Or Dad. We're never going to have any kind of meaningful relationship, but that's okay because I can't expect it. It just didn't work, our family. But that's no one's fault. It's just how it is. We'll live our separate lives and pursue happiness in our own ways. Even you, Mum, when you come out of here again."

I paused. I'd been skirting the thing I wanted to tell Mum ever since I sat down, but I'd run out of other things to say. Also, I was worried that she might wake up soon.

"I never understood why Dad turned away from me, why he made me leave home at sixteen, why he went overseas, why he hardly ever calls. But I think I've worked it out. I was growing up, becoming a woman. Every day, I looked more and more like you when you were young, when you and Dad were first in love. Before your mental illness struck and took you away from us for long periods at a time. I thought he hated me, but that's not true. He just couldn't bear seeing me grow into the woman that you once were, when you were full of life, creative, mysterious, wild and weird—in the best sense, of course—and full of love. Even now, he can hardly bear to spend any time with me. It's not because he hates me. It's because he loved you so much, and I only remind him of what you once were to him."

I stopped playing with my earrings and started twirling my hair, and I got unsteadily to my feet. I looked past my mother, out of the window. The trees swayed gently in the breeze, and I found it peaceful to watch, so I stayed for half a minute before I turned to leave.

At the door, I paused, without looking back. I had one more thing to say. "I'll come again soon, Mum. I promise."

I was about to close the door behind me softly, so as not to disturb her, when I thought I heard something. I thought I heard my mother say, "Chloe, I've always loved you." However, I must have imagined it, for she was asleep. *How the mind plays tricks.*

I grasped the door handle. For a split second, through the gap as I closed the door, I thought I saw my mother looking at me.

I left the hospital, walking at first, as fast as I could, then running. I ran through the corridors and out of the main entrance, and I didn't stop until I reached the road. I don't even know why.

I'd heard about a clandestine therapy group run by a rebel psychology student, and it piqued my interest. It might be just the thing I need to help me visualise where to direct my life from here or, if not, it should at least be interesting to see what other people turn up. Later that day, I followed the directions I'd received over the phone and took the back stairs up to a dingy hallway on the hotel's second floor. This wasn't somewhere that I'd recommend for visitors to stay in Christchurch, unless I didn't like them much. But it was a perfect place to hold a meeting away from prying eyes.

I paused on the landing and looked ahead, trying to determine which door led to the small private meeting room I was looking for. One of the doors opened a few seconds later, and a wiry, ginger-bearded man stepped out. He gazed at me in what was probably a meaningful way. Unfortunately, I couldn't interpret the meaning in his look.

"Are you Bernie?" I asked. Bernie was the guy I'd spoken to on the phone.

"Yes. And you are—Chloe?"

"Yes. How did you know?"

"An educated guess. I'm good at connecting appearances and voices. You look a lot like what I expected after our phone call earlier. And, also, you're the last one to arrive. I'm not expecting anyone else." He grinned.

"Right." Bernie had described himself as 'a renegade Psychology Masters student' who was only loosely associated with academia. He seemed to be developing a thesis based on his own unusual curriculum of study, and was always on the lookout for people to take part in his unsanctioned experiments.

Bernie beckoned me to follow him into the room. "Welcome to our little group, Chloe."

I hesitated in the doorway. The room was quite dark. If it had curtains or blinds, they had been pulled down, and all the lights had been turned off. The only light seeped in from the dingy hallway. In the gloom, I could see the outlines of several other people sitting in chairs scattered around the edges of the room, but I couldn't make out their features. It looked like all the chairs were in pairs around small tables.

"Your seat is over there." Bernie indicated an empty chair against the side wall. "Sorry about the darkness. It's necessary for the experiment."

"Why all the secrecy, Bernie? And why isn't the experiment being held at the university? I don't understand."

"Sit down, and I'll explain."

I made my way slowly to the side of the room in case there was anything hidden that might trip me up. I felt awkward. Maybe I shouldn't have come here. I didn't know what I was getting myself into. Also, the fact that it was on the second floor of an old building wasn't good, just in case of further earthquakes. But I sat down anyway, and Bernie closed the door, blocking out the gloomy light from the hallway, except for a little that seeped underneath the door.

"Okay, welcome, everybody," said Bernie, raising his voice to speak to the whole group. "Firstly, the obligatory health and safety warning. In the event of a major earthquake, I'll switch on the lights, and we all get the hell out of here. Is that clear?"

There was silence. I nodded, even though I realised that was pointless. It was too dark to see what any of the others did, including the person sitting opposite me. That didn't seem to bother Bernie, though. He continued.

"Why the secrecy? Well, it's like this... the university doesn't strictly approve of my course of study. In fact, they banned me for unethical behaviour, but that didn't surprise me, really. My research is pretty cutting-edge, way-out avant-garde. I guess it ruffled a few feathers. Anyway, I'm still going to complete my thesis. I'm sure it'll be fine in the end."

"So that's why your experiments are held off campus," someone said. A male.

"Yes. I can't hold them at the university because of the restraining order. But that doesn't matter. There are always obstacles in the path of those people brave enough to forge new therapeutic techniques such as this. But, at the moment, until my thesis is completed, I feel safer conducting my work without the university's knowledge."

"Why is it so dark?" I asked. "We can't see each other."

"Exactly. That's an important component in the experiment. Remember, this is therapeutic as well as highly experimental. It's important to maintain anonymity, if possible, for complete objectivity. Some groups wear blindfolds, and some groups wear masks. This one is a lights-off group."

"What if we do recognise someone? Will that affect the results of the experiment?" I had to ask the obvious questions.

"Yes, almost certainly, so please tell me later if you do know someone here, and I'll try to factor out the relevant variables when doing the statistical analysis afterwards."

Good luck with that, I thought.

"How many groups do you have?" The same male voice again.

"I can't say, but there are several. It seems that, after the earthquakes, half of Christchurch is either popping antidepressants or sleeping pills, or attending therapy. Even experimental ones like mine."

"So... is it like Group Therapy?" A female voice, from the other side of the room.

"No, not at all. That used to be the fad therapy thirty years ago, but it's highly discouraged now. Apparently, group therapy didn't help anyone and actually led to lots of inappropriate sexual relationships. So it's not that at all. As I said, this is a unique method of therapy that I've developed myself. I call it... Speed Therapy. You're all going to be each other's speed therapists."

Speed Therapy? I thought. Is that something like Speed Dating?

"You might be thinking, 'Is that something like Speed Dating?' And you'd be right. Each of you will have six minutes talking to each of the others. At the beginning, you'll explain your problem briefly to the person sitting opposite you—and by 'briefly' I mean no more than one minute—and then they will do the same. Finally, for the last four minutes of your time, you'll offer advice or potential solutions to each other. Then I'll ring a bell and everyone I designate will move on to someone else they haven't yet talked to, and then you repeat the process with them. Is that clear?"

There were a few 'um's and 'ah's. I understood what Bernie meant, though. The only problem I could foresee was actually being able to find the next table in the gloom.

"You'll pick it up quickly. Once I've rung the bell, I'll guide each of you to your next table. It's too dark in here for you to try to make your own way. That'd just be chaos. I've got a flashlight. Now, shall we start? I'll come around to see each group to make sure you all know what you're doing."

I felt like my head was spinning. I hadn't known what to expect when I signed up for the 'revolutionary therapy experiment', but I wouldn't have guessed that I'd be swapping problems and solutions in the dark for six minutes at a time. It felt surreal. I wondered what Jacqui would say if she knew I was doing this. I'm sure she wouldn't approve. I felt as if I was cheating on my psychotherapist.

I started as a 'client' and described to my 'therapist', who said he was befuddled by the whole situation too, in a minute what I thought my problems were, and that I didn't know where to begin to rebuild my life after everything that's happened to me. I had to talk rapidly to mention even half of it. He seemed to listen attentively to me. After my time was up, he told me his problem.

"It's earthquake-related stress," he said. "Every time there's an aftershock, I tremble. I can't sleep well at night, and I can't get back to sleep after an aftershock bigger than about a 'three'. It's hard to keep up with my study." He went on and on about it. I guess I wasn't being demonstratively empathetic.

Eventually, I asked him what he thought about my situation.

"You're screwed, dude," he said. It didn't sound as if he had much empathy for me either. More like *crapathy*, that attitude of not giving a shit. "Uni dropout, lost most of your savings, dumped by your boyfriend. There's not much you can do. So I can't help you with nothing."

"That's not helpful. Any proper suggestions?"

"I've got nothing. Now, what about my problem. Any ideas?"

"Move to Australia," I said. That was flippant, but it actually would work. Lots of people were jumping across the ditch to escape from the quakes.

We sat in silence after that until the bell went, and I moved on to the next table. If it was going to be like this, I wouldn't stay long.

The next person was a young woman, and I repeated my list of problems to her. She listened intently, reflecting back at times. When it was her turn to speak, she told me that she was addicted to sex.

"I'm a complete nymphomaniac," she confessed. "I can't help it. All I can think about is sex. And the earthquakes make it worse. Whenever there's an aftershock, I want the earth to move for me too."

"Okay... um, I'm not sure I can help with that. Ah, do you have a boyfriend or a husband?"

"No. I'm a lesbian."

I'm definitely not helping with that. "Um, clubs, bars, internet dating..." I ran out of ideas at this point. "Anyway, can you think of anything to help me with my situation?"

"I don't think you have any problems at all," she said. "What you've got is opportunities. A clean slate. Just look forward and go and do whatever you want. You've got no ties, no obligations, no responsibilities."

"I hadn't thought of it like that."

"It's all a matter of perspective. You're not in a bad place at all. In fact, you could—"

The bell rang. I had to move on. I decided I would stay with the group meeting until the end. Perhaps this unusual new therapy might give me some useful ideas after all.

I was surprised to find that the next person I met was Kaperielu, the taxi driver who had rescued me. When he gave me that lovely huge smile of his, his teeth seemed to pick up all the stray light particles in the room, and there was no doubt that it was him in the dark on the other side of the table. I wondered how he could possibly have any problems and yet seem so happy.

"What are you here for, Kaperielu?" I asked. I wasn't sure that I wanted to tell him about all my background, even though he knew me a little, including that I'd recently spent a few days in the psychiatric hospital. However, I knew I could trust him, and that should make it easier. I wondered how he felt about talking to me.

"Hey, is that Chloe? How's it going?"

"Badly." I noticed he had avoided answering my question. "I'm here for, well, everything really. Earthquake stress. I've broken up with my boyfriend. I've dropped out of uni. I went a bit crazy, though I think you know that already, and I lost a lot of money gambling at that time."

"Gambling? Hey, that's my problem too."

"What kind of gambling?" I asked, even though I wondered if it actually mattered.

"Pokie machines. Horses. Dogs. Rugby. It got worse after the quakes. And I'm sleeping in my taxi because I couldn't keep up wif my rent, and the landlord threw me out. I need to stop before I lose everything. The taxi's all I has now."

"Oh. That's not good. Why don't you stop, then, if that's what you want to do?"

He shrugged as if that were a ridiculous question. My eyes had become used to the low level of light by now, and I could just make out his shadowy movement in the dark. "I can't do it. It just pulls me in, every day. I can't stop."

"I stopped. I lost thousands of dollars playing poker when I wasn't in my right mind, and then I gave up. I didn't want to lose any more. So, what's stopping you from giving up, then?"

Kaperielu shook his head meaningfully in a big figure-eight motion. Unfortunately, I couldn't interpret the meaning. Puzzled, I waited for him to say something.

"It's such a great feeling when I win. It's the best feeling in the world."

"But what about when you lose?"

"That's the second best feeling."

I paused while I considered this. "Maybe you should try a different hobby, like reading. Do you read much?"

"Nah. I'm not much of a reader, eh. I'm more of a talker and a driver."

"Well, I don't know how I can advise you how to stop gambling. I just stopped because I wanted to stop. There wasn't any more to it than that. I wish I could get my money back, but I don't know how, and I'm not going to try gambling again because I'll probably just lose the rest."

"Yeah. But someone wins, don't theys? A few people, maybe. But theys don't tell anyone their secrets of how theys do it."

The bell rang. We hadn't actually got anywhere, but just as I got up to be escorted to the next table, a thought occurred to me. A bizarre and somewhat crazy idea, but I don't really have any other kind.

"Talk to me afterwards," I said. "I've got an idea."

The speed therapy meeting lasted another half hour or so. At the conclusion, Bernie asked us, still in the dark, if any of us had felt that it was a waste of time coming along. No one spoke up. I would have if I'd felt that way, but I actually felt better after all that. I don't see how a few minutes of chatting with strangers could do that, but it had. Maybe it was because it made me realise that some people have worse problems than me. But there had to be more to it than that; otherwise, the person with the worst problems wouldn't have felt any better. In fact, they would almost certainly feel worse. So perhaps there is a therapeutic element at work in this after all. Maybe I'd been able to help someone with my naïve suggestions. The lesbian nymphomaniac had helped me, by simply reframing the issues for me, so I no longer felt my problems overburdened me, but had some positive things to think about instead.

And chatting to Kaperielu had given me an idea, which I wanted to follow up on with him.

At the end of the meeting, Bernie said we could go home if we wanted to, or we could stay and chat further, but the experimental part of the meeting was over. He switched on the lights so we could find the door. The sudden light made me blink crazily until I adjusted to it. When I finally felt comfortable enough with the light level, I noticed Kaperielu sitting next to me.

"How was that, eh?" he asked.

"What? Turning on the lights suddenly? It gave me a headache."

"Nah. I meant the meeting. Did ya find it helpful?"

"Yeah, it was useful. Someone helped me see everything in a different way. That's good because usually I get stuck in the same way of thinking about things. It's called perseverative thinking."

"Persev—what?"

"It means ruminating about things over and over again without getting off the same thought track."

"Oh. I dunno if it helps me with my gambling problem. Why did ya wanna talk to me afterwards?"

"I don't have a gambling problem anymore, but I want to get my money back. I've got an idea. It was something you said."

"Yeah? What did I say?"

"You said some people win and keep their methods a secret. That made me realise your problem isn't gambling as such, it's losing. If you were winning, it wouldn't be a problem, would it?"

Kaperielu scratched his head. He appeared to be thinking. "Well, yeah. I s'pose."

"Well, why don't we just ask someone what their secret method is? Then we can learn it and start winning. We can get our money back."

"Nah. Why would anyone tell us their secret? And, anyways, I dunno anyone who wins. Do you?"

"Yeah. I think so. Let's go and have a coffee and talk about it."

The next morning, I waited impatiently for Kaperielu to arrive. My bag was packed and ready. It had my laptop, a refill pad, pens and a digital voice recorder. At 10.14 a.m., while I finished my second coffee and third iced doughnut of the morning, a double toot blared out from the driveway.

I grabbed my bag and hurried outside, keen to get on with my plan. I didn't know if it would work or not, but I'd soon find out. Kaperielu's taxi sat in the driveway, and he gave me a cheery smile and wave. I got into the front passenger seat and put my bag on the floor in front of me.

"Let's go," I said. "I'll give you directions as we drive. It's not far."

"Are you sure about dis?"

"Yes. Just remember, he probably won't be pleased to see me. We might have to leave in a hurry if it all goes wrong."

"I'll leave the keys in the car," said Kaperielu. He started the engine and skilfully backed the car out onto the roadway.

"That way, then left at the corner."

Three minutes later, we pulled up outside Carlos's Corner Shop. Like most dairies, it was open long hours, but customers were few because the supermarkets are always much cheaper. It was the kind of shop that served people in a hurry, drive-by traffic, and a few loyal customers. We walked in, triggering the bell that announced our arrival.

Carlos sat behind the counter, a baseball cap on his head, his legs propped up on a stool and a laptop balanced precariously on two boxes of salt 'n' vinegar chips. Even from the shop doorway, I could make out a poker game on his laptop screen. I guessed that this was what Carlos did most days when he wasn't serving customers. He looked up with a smile when the bell rang, but when he saw me, he jumped to his feet, his smile replaced by a scowl, and waved his arms about.

"You again! What are you doing here, young lady? You

tried to rob my shop, and you stole my car—it was you, no? And you dare return? *Fíyete!* Go away!"

"Did ya do that?" asked Kaperielu. "Steal his car?"

"Um, yes. For a while. But I told the police where I left it." I strode up to the counter. Carlos leaned forward over it. I could see, and smell, that he hadn't brushed his teeth that morning. "I'm sorry about those things. I wasn't in my right mind at the time. I was having a manic episode and wasn't really thinking about what I was doing."

"Ah... Carlos does not know what that is, but the *astinomía* did tell me that you were a little bit cuckoo at the time. So, why have you returned? Has the young lady come to apologise?"

"Yes. I am sorry, like I said. And I'm fine now. I was in hospital for a few days."

"Yeah, that's right," said Kaperielu. "I picked her up in my taxi. She had bags and stuff. Looked like she'd been there a while, eh."

"Anyway, I'm perfectly rational now. I won't do anything odd. Or stupid. Well, no more than usual. I'm not here to rob you or steal your car again. I just want to talk to you for a few minutes. Maybe get your help with something."

"Yeah," said Kaperielu. He grinned widely and nodded in a friendly manner, extending his hand. "We'd really appreciate your help. And we can help ya in return."

Carlos looked from me to Kaperielu's beaming smile and his outstretched hand. His scowl melted away. Probably he couldn't keep up such a cold stare in the force of Kaperielu's warm and friendly demeanour. Slowly, a smile appeared on his face, the enormous smile I remembered from the first time I came into his shop. He took Kaperielu's hand and shook it. "Carlos will listen. I will," he said. "And who are you, my new friend?"

The two of them smiled broadly at each other like two cats let loose in a cream-bottling factory. Kaperielu introduced himself as a taxi driver and a friend of mine. For a minute or two, they seemed to forget about me as they exchanged social pleasantries, which I thought was kind of strange given the circumstances of Kaperielu obviously being with me, and Carlos not happily disposed towards me. But they both seemed to enjoy it. Then Carlos turned his attention back to me and raised his eyebrows.

"So... tell me what this is about, and why you think Carlos might help you."

"Will you teach us how to play poker? Really well, like you do. You're 'Carlos The Greek', right?" He nodded as I continued without a pause. "I know you're good. When I was manic, I played internet poker and lost a lot of money. You won most of it. It was a high stakes game."

"I play a lot of internet poker. *Né*, I'm good, or at least good enough to take some money out of the game. But the game is—how you say?—anonymous. I could not have known if one of the other players was you, or if it was a guy in Hong Kong or Athens or anywhere. I suppose you want to ask Carlos for your money back? Sorry to disappoint you, my pretty young friend, but the game does not operate that way."

"I'm not asking you to give me my money back. I'm asking you to teach us how to play poker well so we can both win back the money we lost gambling online."

Carlos looked from me to Kaperielu, who was still smiling broadly, and back again. "You said you could help me. What did you mean by that?"

"I can build a website for you, for your shop or whatever. Or for a friend or family member of yours. You can charge them for it if you want, but you just have to teach us how to play. And I can help in the shop too."

"I can deliver stuff for ya all over Christchurch, eh," said Kaperielu. "Between fares. If you'll teach me when I'm not driving my cab."

"I do not sell goods all over Christchurch," said Carlos. "There are only the local customers who stop by for milk or bread or the newspaper sometimes. Not much else. My shop makes a loss. That's why I play poker—to make some money."

"I'll make a website for you and get it onto the first page of Google for relevant keyword searches. Then you'll have customers from all over Christchurch, I promise."

"Yeah, an' I'll get my bros and couzies and their mates to come and buy their stuff here, eh. I has a lot of couzies, and theys has a lot of mates too."

Carlos flicked his attention from me to Kaperielu and back again. It was like we were two ends of a tennis court and there was a game going on in the space between us. "The two of you are serious, no? You want Carlos to teach you how to win at poker?"

"Yes, absolutely," I said.

"And you will help in the shop, no?"

"Yes. I'll do that. If you teach us when we have time. At least three hours a day."

Carlos smiled broadly, just as I remembered, and extended his hand, this time towards me. "My new friends, you both have a deal."

CHAPTER **T**WELVE

I was back in the Red Zone, some indefinable time after the earthquake, but I couldn't wake up, although I know I stirred in my sleep. In this dream—or nightmare, if it became one— I was alone. It was dawn. I was amongst the ruined and abandoned buildings, walking down the centre of Colombo Street towards the crumbled cathedral, not far from the centre of town. My foot brushed loose bits of rubble as I went along, and in my dream I could hear them skittering along the ground as if they were real.

After a few moments, I became aware that I wasn't simply a passenger in this dream. I had some control over where I could go and what I could do. With this realisation, I turned to walk east, away from the wreckage of what had been before and towards the reborn sun.

A chilly gust of wind surprised me, and I gasped, swallowing a mouthful of cold air that made my dream-self shiver. I blinked and found myself in the same café that I'd visited in my previous earthquake dream. The same cold coffee and piece of mouldy cake sat undisturbed on the same table. I quickly looked around for the—I didn't know what to call them—who talked to me in the other dream, but they were gone. Perhaps their family had come back for them after all.

I spent a dream-minute or two trying to find a way out

of that café without success, then remembered that this was my dream, and I could choose where to go and what to do. I closed my dream-eyes, wished I was outside again and, when I opened them, found myself in a hazel wood. How that happened, I don't know, because I had never imagined such a place, let alone visited one, and I wouldn't recognise a hazel tree unless it was clearly labelled as such.

I dream-walked along a twisted dirt path through the wood, recalling everything I'd ever read or heard about hazel trees, trying to figure out if they had some relevance to my dream. I remembered that hazel trees are said to confer wisdom and secret knowledge, and the wood from them is said to have magical properties and protect from evil. The wood certainly appeared a magical place: quiet with beams of sunlight piercing through the leafy veil overhead. I felt content there, secure in the feeling that I was on a purposeful and transformative journey.

The path straightened, widened and emerged into a sheltered clearing. In the centre was a quirky old cottage. I paused, gazing at it, drinking in its tranquil beauty. I just knew that, if I ever lived in a cottage in the woods, it would be exactly like the one in front of me. Everything about it was ideal for me; its aspect, size, colour, layout, features.

I mounted the wooden steps as if I owned the place. The door was ajar, and I went in to a welcoming room in which a fire crackled merrily in the hearth. There was a sturdy table and a single chair in the centre of the room, and two comfy armchairs side by side against one wall. Immediately, it felt familiar in some undefinable way, but not because I'd ever been there.

One corner of the room was gloomy, and I walked towards it, my dream-boots making no sound on the wooden floor. A narrow stairway was there, almost hidden, and I descended it slowly and a little fearfully. The steps ended at a solid door that I knew was locked, but somehow I pushed it open effortlessly. I emerged into a cellar that should have been almost completely dark, but was mysteriously illuminated as if by moonlight, though there were no windows. There were indistinct pictures on the walls that reminded me of my mother and of myself as a child.

The only other furniture in the room was a tall hazelwood bookcase overflowing with books. I walked up to it and examined them, but I couldn't read their titles or even discern if they had any. Most were large, precious, leather-bound books. I reached out and took a heavy one from its place on the shelf, and it sent shivers up my spine as if I were exposed to a chilly gust of wind. Why I had picked this particular book, I did not know, but I instinctively knew in my dream that it had the utmost significance to me, and yet had the potential to be deeply terrifying.

I leafed through the pages, glancing at swirly dark characters that I couldn't decipher, and dark abstract inkblot pictures like the ones my psychiatrist occasionally shows me. Though I could make no sense of them individually, I knew this book related to my life—specifically, to the past, and to things in the past that have troubled me and caused me pain. With this realisation, my fingers started to burn as if the book was on fire, and I almost dropped it, but I knew that if I did, I would wake up, and I wasn't going to let that happen.

Through the dream-pain, I held the book in my right hand and began tearing at the pages with my left. I have never in real life defaced or damaged any book, but in my dream I tore at the pages ferociously, ripped them out in chunks as if my life depended upon it and scattered them in the air, where they disintegrated and vanished without trace. I methodically destroyed the contents of the book, and it became lighter in terms of both weight and colouration. At the same time, a corresponding weight seemed to lift from my shoulders, my mind and my heart. Finally, there was nothing left of the tome except the leather cover, and I put it back on the shelf where I had found it.

Another book caught my attention, but I do not know why, because it looked unremarkable on the shelf. However, when I withdrew it, I saw it had a vague, ethereal quality, and it was as light as air. It opened of its own accord, and the pages ruffled by under my intense gaze. Every one of them was blank. They yearned to be filled with life—my life. I understood instantly that this book represented my unwritten future and I, alone, was the would-be author of my destiny. I wanted to seize that book and hold it close to my heart and take it away with me, but in my dream I knew it could not leave the bookcase in the cellar. Reluctantly, yet full of renewed hope, I put the book back on the shelf.

I returned upstairs. The room hadn't changed, but it somehow felt more homely, and I examined it thoughtfully. It struck me that the objects in the room represented my friends—my new and true family. The bright, warm fire was Robert; the sturdy table and chair was Stef; and even Carlos and Kaperielu were there in the form of the comfy armchairs.

I stayed a while longer, feeling completely at home there, and when I closed my eyes in the dream, in real life I woke up.

I created an appealing website for Carlos's dairy the next morning and, with a bit of search engine optimisation, soon had it prominently displayed on relevant searches and in pop-up ads. I sent out spider programs onto the internet to track down anyone in the Greek community in New

Zealand and Australia who had an online presence and emailed them details of Carlos's specially imported Greek goods. I also targeted community groups, schools and anyone I could think of who might be interested. By the end of the day, I'd done it all, website, marketing, the lot.

I was pretty *gruntled* with my work, and went downstairs to the kitchen, smiling. It was good timing, for Stef was about to serve up dinner from the slow cooker.

"What's up with you?" she asked as I set the table. "You look as pleased as punch."

"What are you talking about?" I asked, puzzled. I'd never properly understood the meaning of most idioms.

"I meant, why are you so pleased with yourself?" She smiled strangely and lowered her voice to a whisper before continuing. "Have you found a new boyfriend?"

"No, of course not, Stef! Why would you think that? Are you serious?"

She shrugged. "Not really. Well, is it a job, then?"

"No. I am working on a new project though. If it works out, I won't need to get a job."

"Oh, good on you. I guess you must be writing that bestseller after all."

"Um..." How could I explain to Stef that I was planning to become a professional poker player? Luckily, I was saved from denial and further explanation by Robert's entry into the kitchen.

"Chloe! I've been home most of the afternoon, and this is the first time I've seen you. Have you been busy?"

"Yes." That was all I wanted to say for now, I decided. My cell phone emitted the *Star Trek* teleporter sound to signal a text message had come through. It was Kaperielu. He was coming to pick me up in ten minutes.

"Oh. I've got to go out. I'll talk to you guys later, okay?" I grabbed the nearest steaming plate of casserole and went upstairs with it. I wanted to double-check a couple of things with the website before I showed it to Carlos.

Though I felt a little queasy, I was also starving. However, I only managed to eat half of my dinner before Kaperielu arrived, honking twice to let me know he was parked outside. I rushed downstairs.

"There's a taxi outside, Chloe," said Stef as I rushed through the kitchen. "It looks like the same taxi driver who picked us up from the hospital."

"Yes, I know," I said. "See you later." I hurried out of the door, my laptop tucked under my arm. Both Stef and Robert knew that I couldn't normally afford taxis, being unemployed and a uni dropout, so I knew they would ask me later what I was doing. How could I tell them that Kaperielu was giving me lifts to our private poker *masterclasses*? After losing so much money when I was manic, I didn't think I could tell them this—yet—though I knew I would have to give them the truth sometime.

"*Kalespéra*," said Carlos as we entered the shop. "My day has been busy. It has. Plenty of Samoans stopping by for things on their way to and from work. Your cousins, Kaperielu, no?"

"Yeah. I put the word around, said theys be helping me out if they buy theirs daily stuff from your shop, if theys anywhere near."

He beamed. "Excellent! I am impressed. It was my best sales day since the earthquake."

"I've got something to show you, too," I said, placing my laptop on the shop counter and moving around to stand next to Carlos. Kaperielu came over and stood next to me, making it a bit of a squeeze with the three of us squashed in between the cash register and Carlos's portable television, which seemed permanently tuned to the channel showing the World Series of Poker.

I demonstrated the website to Carlos, including the ability to order and pay online, the map and contact details and a description of the unusual merchandise on offer. Carlos stared at it, his cigar dangling tentatively between open lips. Finally, once I'd finished showing him, he said, "You did this much today?"

"It didn't take me all day, of course. Just the morning. I did some advertising for you and sent some emails in the afternoon. You should have a few online orders coming through any time now."

Carlos checked his laptop and chuckled. "My pretty little friend, you are right. There are three orders already for *calamari*, olive oil and *dolmades*. Thank you!"

He turned and grabbed me in a giant bear hug before I could move out of the way, though, with the lack of room, I doubted I could have escaped anyway. His enormous fat lips, cigar and all, closed on my left cheek for a quick kiss. "*Efharistó!* Thank you!" he reiterated.

When he let go of me, I staggered backwards, falling into Kaperielu, who appeared to be trying not to laugh. Carlos seized his hand and shook it vigorously. "Thank you both!" he said.

"So...you'll teach us how to play poker...and win?"

"I will, most certainly. It will be my pleasure."

Carlos was true to his word. Over the next ten days, I spent almost every waking minute at his corner shop. Kaperielu dropped by between fares, and after he had finished for the day. Carlos taught us everything from the basics to advanced strategy.

"Online poker is not the same as face-to-face poker," he instructed. "You are playing the person, not only their cards, but the person. Online, you cannot see them. You have to figure out what kind of person they are by how they play. And remember," he cautioned, "if after thirty minutes you do not know who the fool at the table is, it's you!"

Carlos was a remarkably gifted teacher, who obviously loved the game and delighted in sharing his knowledge with us. I learned to master the game quickly, even with my dyscalculia. Kaperielu took longer to gain the knowledge and skills, but Carlos patiently educated him. We practised for hours. We watched poker tournaments online and on television with Carlos's constant running commentary advising on the tactics and strategies being employed by the world's best players. I took screeds of notes and, once I got home late in the evening, distilled them into rules and then into computer code.

One evening, when I got home at 10.14 p.m., Robert was sitting at the kitchen table, reading one of his interminable economics books, evidently waiting for me. I don't know why he reads such books. From what I understand, if you ask a dozen economists for an opinion, you'll get twenty different ones. As far as I was concerned, economics existed only to make weather forecasting and astrology look good.

"Chloe, you've been out every night for nearly two weeks, and you're never here in the day either. What's going on? Have you got a job with long hours? I know you're not back at university."

"I'm working on a special project," I said. I laid my laptop on the kitchen table and went to the cupboard to grab a mug and the jar of coffee.

"You smell awful. Have you been smoking?"

"No, but I've been with someone who does." I spun around, brandishing a teaspoon like a mini rapier. "What difference does it make to you anyway? We've split up, remember? I don't have to tell you where I am or what I'm doing or when I'll be home."

Robert made a strange moaning sound. Probably from anxiety. He's never been good at any kind of conflict. Even a hint of an argument would cause him to scurry away for the safety of a quiet place. "I've been worried about you."

"Well, I'm fine. You weren't worried when I was going manic, were you? Though I suppose you didn't realise. But that's when I needed your help. I don't need it now." I turned back to finish making my drink, pursing my lips. Maybe I'd been too harsh. Robert had always been kind to me. The fact that he hadn't noticed when I went off the rails wasn't because he didn't care, it was because he didn't know. I knew that. But I also knew that he hadn't forgiven me for the way I'd behaved, for my betrayal of him.

I lifted my mug to my lips and turned around, unsure of what to do or say next. Robert stared at me silently, implacably. I couldn't read his expression or determine what he was thinking.

"What are you thinking?" I asked. It's usually the only reliable way to find out.

"Is that taxi driver your new boyfriend?"

I stared at him, stunned that he might think that. "No, he's a friend, that's all."

"You go out with him every night." A statement of fact. Probably not an accusation.

"Well, yes, but we're studying together, working together."

"On your special project?"

"Yes."

"Are you going to tell me what it is?"

I took a long, slow sip of my coffee while I gave that some thought. Why wouldn't I tell Robert? He's still my friend, after all. I used to share all my projects and plans with him.

"I'm angry at you," I said. I'd only just realised it that moment. "I'm angry because you didn't help me when I needed it. I was getting out of control, and you didn't notice. You didn't protect me. I did crazy things, and then you didn't forgive me for them, even though I couldn't stop myself at the time."

"I know," he muttered.

"Luckily, Stef saw the signs eventually and helped me before it got any worse."

"I just thought you were excited about something new, some new idea of yours…and you were stressed by the earthquakes at the same time. I did not know that it was more than that. Did you not realise, yourself, that you were out of control?"

"No, I fucking didn't." I noticed that Robert's speech had reverted to his old pedantic style. I knew that meant he was probably stressed, upset or afraid of something. I still felt angry, though, and not willing to calm down yet.

He was silent for a while, seated as still as a statue, staring at me with an expression that I could not fathom, even though I knew him well. I sipped my drink. It seemed to help calm me, so I finished it.

"I was wrong," he finally said. "I mean, it was wrong of me to treat you like that. I know it was not your fault. Of course I know that. I just did not see it at the time."

I would have thrown my coffee at him, except the cup was now empty. Men could be so frustrating! Especially Aspie men. Emotions surged through me, racing past my consciousness before I could determine what they even were. I felt weak, confused, nauseated. I put the cup on the bench, put my hands over my face and discovered that I was already crying, softly at first, then emitting loud sobs. I didn't even know why.

"Are you okay?" Robert asked after half a minute or so. I shook my head, unable to respond yet. I wanted his arms around me. I wanted to feel safe and secure in his gentle embrace. I wanted him to forgive me, and I didn't want to be angry at him anymore.

After another half a minute, he asked, "Would you like a drink of water?"

"Oh, just give me a hug, will you?"

I didn't hear him get up, but moments later I felt his arms encircling me, pulling me in. I rested my head on his shoulder and pawed at his chest with my left hand, indicating that I wanted him to hug me tightly. Deep pressure. That was what I needed—deep pressure. It's so calming and reassuring.

We stayed like that without speaking, swaying slightly, for a long time. Perhaps for about three and a half minutes, though I don't know exactly. I let out a massive sigh and pulled away from him.

"Robert," I said. "I think I'm pregnant."

CHAPTER THIRTEEN

"How do you know?" asked Robert. "Have you taken a test?"

"I haven't taken a test. I don't know for sure... I just feel that I might be. It would explain the nausea I've been having. I was on the contraceptive pill before the earthquake, but I lost those in the house as well...and I know they don't work all the time for everyone anyway."

"When? Who?" gasped Robert, stepping away from me. His face was a sea of emotions, his features rising and falling in undecipherable rhythms. I had to look away.

"I don't know that either," I whispered. "Can't we wait and see?"

"No. The baby's not going to announce whom its father is when it's born, is it? Is it me? Or is it your shower fling?"

"It wasn't a fling! I was manic!"

"I know. Sorry. I was just teasing you this time. But it is important. Look, let's think about this logically. First, you need to find out if you are actually pregnant. You can go to the doctor and have a test. Then, if you are pregnant, you have to find out whose baby it is. Is it mine? Or his? You'll have to find out somehow."

"I know." I'd already worked all that out, of course. It's the obvious course of action. What troubled me, though, is why I suddenly thought I might be pregnant. Was it that irrational phenomenon called 'intuition'? Or was my unconscious mind insidiously punishing me for my sexual misadventure by planting this terrifying thought in my conscious mind? I was no way ready yet to care for a baby, whoever the father was. Not yet.

"Are you okay, Chloe?" This was the closest Robert would get to asking me how I actually felt about my suspected pregnancy.

I moved closer to him. Robert wrapped his arms around me, and once again I felt safe. *He's forgiven me after all.*

"I'm not okay, no. I'm frightened. It's not safe to get pregnant while I'm on the meds I'm taking. And I don't know how I would cope with a baby anyway." I paused before asking, "Are you okay?"

"I don't know. Let's wait until you've had the test and we know what the situation is."

It was late now. I was tired after all the work I'd been doing at Carlos's shop, and I told Robert that I needed to go to sleep. With all the programming and reading I'd been doing as well as the shop work and poker training, I hadn't had more than six hours of sleep a night for ten days. He bade me goodnight.

I went to my bedroom and started my laptop. It took me an hour to enter all of the day's training information into my program, and by then, I was mentally and physically exhausted. I turned off the light and went to bed.

I fell asleep almost immediately, but before I did, I wondered if Robert and I would be sleeping together again soon.

I hadn't told Stef yet, and rather than risk a further discussion with Robert about my suspected pregnancy over breakfast, I stayed in my room until I heard the bang of the door behind him as he left for university, and the spluttering of The Frog as Stef left for work. Only then did I rush downstairs to devour two pieces of toast.

Then I phoned the doctor's surgery to make an appointment to see Doctor Penny. Unfortunately, Friday was her day off, so I made an appointment for early on Monday. I didn't want to wait that long, but I knew I'd be uncomfortable seeing someone else, so next week would have to do. For a few moments, I considered getting one of those do-it-yourself kits from the pharmacy, but decided against it. Even if they are 99% accurate, I might do it wrong anyway, and overall that's too much uncertainty for me. It would only make me worry.

I intended to spend most of the day at Carlos's dairy, but first I needed to do something else.

I went to Café Gorgon, about ten minutes' walk away. An attractive young woman with red-streaked black hair wrote down my takeaway coffee order, and then walked to the barista to give him the slip of paper. The barista serving at the moment was Angelo, just as I'd hoped. The woman smiled at him and ran her hand down his muscled arm before she returned to the till to take an order for an old lady.

I strode over. "Hello, Angelo," I said. I assumed he was making my coffee. No one else was waiting for one.

"Oh! I didn't see you there. Chloe, isn't it? Ah... how's things?"

"Pretty shit, really. How's things with you?" I puzzled over how he hadn't seen me at the counter, only a few metres away. He hadn't been busy with anything when I made my order.

"Great! Couldn't be better. Ah... it's great to see you again. Yeah, great. Well, I'll have your coffee ready for you in a moment. Would you like to sit down, and I'll bring it over when it's ready?"

"No."

He coughed. I stood directly in front of his area of the counter and watched as he made my drink. He was remarkably fast at it, almost as if he wanted to serve me as quickly as possible. I wasn't quite sure what to say, but I'd decided to wait until I got my coffee before saying anything. After all, I'd paid for it.

He handed it to me across the counter. I noticed he'd forgotten to give me a napkin and the two little sweeties that usually accompany a coffee. Perhaps only dine-in customers get them. "Is there anything else I can do for you?" he asked in a low voice, his brown eyes lifting to meet mine for the first time and lingering.

"Well, yes, there is, actually."

He smiled and raised an eyebrow but didn't say anything. Out of the corner of my eye, I saw the old lady sidling over to wait for her drink to be made. Red-streaked-hair Girl stood at the till, glaring in my direction.

"You can pay me child support for the next eighteen years."

The colour drained out of Angelo's face, leaving it the hue of overcooked spaghetti left on a plate for hours, cold and unappetising. "That's not possible."

"Of course it is. The government can take it out of your pay."

"No. No. I mean, it's nothing to do with me—"

"What's all this?" demanded the young woman,

appearing at Angelo's side, her face matching the crimson streaks in her hair.

"The baby might be yours. We did have sex in the showers. Don't you remember?"

"What!" shrieked the young woman. "When was this?"

I told her the date, though I didn't see why she wanted to know.

"It can't be mine!" protested Angelo.

"So you admit sleeping with her!"

"Cor Blimey," said the old lady behind me. "This is better than Shortland Street on the telly."

"There wasn't any sleep involved," I said. "Just three minutes' shagging. In the communal showers."

"What!" The young woman raised her voice and her hand at the same time. She brought her fist down on Angelo's chest. "You bastard!"

"It's not mine!" he protested again. "It can't be! I've had—what do you call it?—the snip."

I had to check that I understood this. "Do you mean that you've had a vasectomy? At your age?"

"Yes," said Angelo, taking another pounding from the young woman, with her other hand this time. "The snip. No *bambinos* anymore. Not possible. I already have four children in three different countries. I wanted no more!"

He is a complete dick, then. I'm glad he can't possibly be the father. If I'm pregnant, that is. I turned and walked away, taking a sip from my takeaway coffee. Behind me, the young woman shouted at Angelo again. I passed through the open café doors and heard the old lady say, "Excuse me? What about my single-shot latte?"

Somehow I doubted that Angelo would be able to make it for her in the immediate future.

I drank my coffee as I walked, then discarded the takeaway cup in a handy litter bin before walking on to Carlos's dairy. There were several cars parked outside, which was now usual for this time of the day, it being the end of the morning rush as people stopped to buy snacks and newspapers on their way to work. I entered the shop. The bell rang behind me, which I found quite irritating now. No one could walk in or out without the damn thing going off.

There were several people in the shop, some Samoan, and others whom I presumed to be Greek. Four of them were lined up, waiting to be served. I hurried over to join Carlos behind the counter so I could help the next customer, but before I could do so, he thrust a tray containing two drinks, two steak pies and some cigarettes at me.

"This one is for outside," he said.

I went out through the back door with it because it was quicker than trying to thread my way through the throng of Samoans between me and the front door with the laden tray. Outside, on a sunny patio around the side of the shop, sat some tables and chairs that Carlos had set up a few days ago, creating a small outdoor dining area, because he'd diversified into providing café food now in addition to the usual milk, bread and newspapers. An elderly man beckoned to me from one of the tables, smiling. He and his friend were 'regulars', coming every sunny day to sit in the warmth, play backgammon and partake of Carlos's hospitality.

I went back inside and helped with the other customers. Once they'd all departed, Carlos turned to me and flashed his enormous smile. "It is a marvel," he said. "You are a marvel, my pretty young friend. And your Samoan friend, too. My shop has never been busier, and now I have a café as well. It is all thanks to you two. It is."

I smiled. "It's a fair trade for what you're teaching us."

Kaperielu turned up at that moment. He explained that he'd done a night shift, then gone home and had four hours' sleep.

Carlos unfolded his card table and set it up in the back room. He positioned his laptop on it and started up a poker computer game. It wasn't live over the internet so we couldn't be fleeced by professionals, but he'd set the skill level of the computer-generated players a little higher each day. We practised the skills he'd taught us all day, and he complimented us on playing correctly after each hand, win or lose, except for when he had to hurry back into the shop to serve a customer.

"You are nearly ready," he said, beaming. "Both of you. Kaperielu, you are much improved in the last three days. Chloe, I do believe you have memorised all of the standard starting plays. Well done."

I nodded. *Of course I have.*

At half-past-nine in the evening, we stopped for the night, and Carlos closed up his shop. Kaperielu gave me a lift home, tooting farewell as he drove away after leaving me at the front gate.

I went inside. Again, Robert was waiting for me. I was exhausted, though, and actually didn't want to talk to him until I'd had a quiet sit-down for a while.

"We should talk," he said, clearly oblivious to my desires. "Did you see the doctor?"

"No, she wasn't in today. I'm going to see her on Monday."

"Have you been out with that taxi driver again?"

"What is this? Twenty questions? I'm too tired to talk

now," I said, walking past him. "And I'm not actually going out with him. I'm just going with him to—a place. That's all. Not 'out'."

"Your special project," he muttered.

"Yes. Oh, by the way," I said, pivoting at the base of the stairs. "If I'm pregnant, the baby's yours. Definitely yours. So don't you worry about that anymore. I'm going to my room now. Good night."

"Don't worry about it?" I heard him say as I climbed the stairs. I still had an hour's work ahead of me, refining the rules in my computer program with the new information I'd learned today before I could go to sleep.

Robert knocked on my door at 8.14 a.m. the next morning, Saturday, and barged in without waiting for a response.

"Chloe, this has been worrying me all night. You have to tell me."

I raised my head from the pillow. I'm pretty sure I groaned, but I was actually too tired to notice. "Tell you what?"

"What's going on? You're out every day, all day, and half the night. You go somewhere with that taxi driver, I'm sure of it. And you might be pregnant."

"Those last two things aren't connected in any way, Robert."

He sat on the edge of my bed. "What's this project you're working on? Why haven't you told me? I might be able to help."

"Give me a minute to wake up." My head swirled with confusion. I hadn't told Robert—or Stef —because I didn't want them to know I was getting involved with poker again. I was sure they would try to warn me off. Also, I didn't want to tell Robert because we'd broken up. Maybe that is a childish motive, I don't know, but it is how I felt regardless. But now we are back together—*aren't we?*—I ought to tell him. And, of course, with his economics and *mathemagical* brain, he may be able to help.

"The taxi driver is Kaperielu, a friend. We made a deal with an expert poker player to teach us how to play properly so we could win back our gambling losses."

An NS person might have replied, 'Really?' or 'No kidding?' or even 'No shit?' because this plan would likely sound absurd to them, but not Robert. He understood, accepted and wanted details.

"What kind of poker? How long has he been teaching you?"

I insisted upon Robert getting breakfast in bed for me before I told him any more. I couldn't ignore such exceptional leverage as this. He returned a few minutes later, and I explained all that he wanted to know while enjoying hot toast and coffee.

"Interesting," he said. For Robert, that counts as truly opening up and baring his emotions to the world.

"I'm going to win my money back, I'm confident. I'm not so good with numbers, but I know all of the strategies now. Carlos says I'm almost ready to go online and play."

"You know, you would do better if the three of you played as a team."

"What?" I didn't understand this.

"I mean, if you each play your own hands, but you know what cards you all have, you'll have an advantage over everyone else. Whoever's got the strongest hand continues, and the others fold. Also, you'd know some of the cards that your opponents will not be able to draw."

"Is that legal?"

"I don't know," admitted Robert. "Maybe not. I only thought of it as an academic argument, really. A way of turning the odds in the favour of your team."

"You're a genius! I never thought of that. Of course, we'd have to log on from different locations, different IP addresses, and just play short sessions, so the online casinos won't have a chance to figure out what's going on, but it might just work!"

"But I don't know if it's actually allowed, or even legal—"

"Legal by whose laws? Some of the online poker businesses have their servers in places like Gibraltar, South America or the Caribbean. In places like that, probably anything goes. And who cares?" I didn't, anyway.

I got out of bed, almost spilling the rest of my coffee in my haste, and gave Robert a huge kiss on the mouth. He smiled and hugged me.

"Chloe…"

"Yes?"

"Surely, you don't want to spend all your time playing poker on the internet, do you? That wouldn't leave much time for…for anything else. For anyone else."

I pulled myself back from him. "Of course not. I won't have to spend any time at it. I've been programming my computer to play for me. I've put all the rules into an artificial intelligence program, augmented by a neural network so it will learn and improve…and I can do the same for Kaperielu and Carlos, and the computers can play together as a team, like you suggested. I won't have to spend any time doing it. I'll be able to do whatever I want while the computers play."

"And what is that? What is it you want?" I noticed an edge, a tension, in Robert's voice. I wasn't sure what it meant, though.

"Are we—are we back together? You know, as a couple? No matter what happens?"

"Yes, Chloe. Yes, we are. If you want. No matter what happens."

I pulled him close and *pashed* him fervently. "I want. I want to spend my time with you."

"I'm ninety-nine point nine percent excited about that."

"Me too."

"Hey, I wonder if we have a baby—either now or sometime in the future—if it would be an Aspie."

"I think so, Robert. The genetics favour it. And you know what? I don't just think so—I hope so." I smiled at him. "But I'd rather it wasn't now."

The weekend was the slowest two days I could remember ever experiencing. Now that I had the idea that I *might* be pregnant, it was extremely difficult to put it out of my mind. Even though Robert kept reminding me not to dwell on the situation or worry until after the test, I couldn't help myself. But Monday did eventually arrive, and I did go to see Doctor Penny and had the test.

It was negative.

I breathed a huge sigh of relief at hearing that. At last, I felt free of stress. Finally, I felt empowered to take control of my life. What a great feeling.

EPILOGUE

There's a new normal in Quake City. Like everyone else, I'm getting used to the changed landscape and the changed people. Sometimes it's hard to remember exactly what Christchurch was like before the February quake.

We've lost our famous cathedral, but gained a leaning tower. The Hotel Chancellor seems to tip over a little more each day, though perhaps that is merely my imagination. Many landmarks are gone, especially the old buildings that have been there my entire life and for decades before. Travelling around Christchurch is surreal. It's familiar, it's home, but it's so different than it was. Tanks and soldiers surround the CBD where, even on the fringes, it looks like a war zone. Traffic is always heavy with people taking yet another detour around closed roads, driving slowly through multitudinous roadworks on streets randomly peppered with potholes and humps indicated by green painted circles.

Then there are all the new things that we now accept as normal. Water tankers. Port-a-loos, one or two every block in some areas. Chemical toilet disposal units squatting on the footpaths like mini artillery posts. Signs saying 'Slow down—our houses are shaking'.

A change of population as hordes of people leave Christchurch forever, and demolition teams move in.

Yeah, that's the new normal.

When I explained Robert's idea to Carlos, he became animated and excited. I think he saw it as a new challenge.

It took me a while to complete the program and network the computers together. First, we had to buy one for Kaperielu, because all he owned was his taxi and whatever stuff he had in the boot. And he had to park outside the library or wherever else he could find free wifi access whenever we put the computers to work.

And the program did work. With Carlos's strategies programmed as rules and my computer expertise, the program turned our fortunes around, slowly but steadily. Riches didn't gush in, but they flowed steadily at more than a trickle. We were going to get rich slowly. Though Kaperielu never contributed much to the system itself, I owed him for saving me that day when that tagger and his friends were chasing me, and this was my way of repaying him. After a while, he could afford a place to live and drove his taxi simply for pleasure, usually not even charging his passengers. Carlos traded up to a mini supermarket, employed staff and spent most of his days playing backgammon with his Greek pals.

I went with Stef and Ingrid, who came down from Nelson for a few days, to the special earthquake service for the dead. I felt I needed to go so I could say farewell to Marinda in some tangible way. Stef felt the same, I think, and we both cried on Ingrid's shoulders during the event.

Robert and I have made a pact always to watch out for each other with our medications. It's simple, really; we both promised to try to be more aware of each other's moods and level of activity, especially if one of us changes the type or the dosage of our meds. There won't be any excuses like,

'I thought you were just stressed out', or whatever. If one of us acts uncharacteristically, the other will phone the doctor for an urgent appointment. Stef will keep a watchful eye on us as well, and Carlos and Kaperielu, whom I finally told about my mental disorders and ASD, will monitor me too. All in all, I feel pretty safe now, free to be myself, knowing that my friends—or my new family, as I now think of them—will step in to steady me if I waver off my true path. I know what I need to do to be myself and stay healthy, and I've accepted that now.

It's a tremendous relief when you finally realise you don't have to be so critical of yourself all the time.

"Be who you are and say what you feel, for those who mind don't matter, and those who matter don't mind."— some anonymous genius. Possibly Dr. Seuss.

I've decided to leave my diary at this point. It seems the right thing to do. Mainly because I think that my life is back on track. I've overcome a lot. I feel like a changed person now, and whole again. I believe that enough has changed for me to want to close the chapter on the past. My problems, like the earthquakes, seem to be behind me now.

One of the changes I'm making is that I'm going to visit my mother every week from now on, and read her part of my diary each time. I don't know how much she'll listen to, or understand, but if she comprehends even a small part of it, she'll see a little better who I am and what my life is like. Maybe she'll react to, or comment on, some of the events I read to her from my diary. That would be a positive thing. A genuine emotional reaction to something that happened to me. That's got to be better than her simply imagining things and freaking out.

I also wonder what I should do next. Rebuilding my

relationship with Robert will take priority, naturally. But I would still have time to spare, as I hadn't returned to uni.

Perhaps I'll have time to write that bestseller after all. I hope so, anyway.

ABOUT THE AUTHOR

I've been writing off and on approximately forever. I'm middle-aged in a chronological sense, but young at heart. My favourite genres to read are speculative fiction and YA, but I also read some contemporary and some non-fiction books. My favourite author is Connie Willis, but I mostly read indie authors nowadays. My other interests include editing, hanging out with other writers, walking, playing backgammon, dancing Ceroc and spending time with my two boys. I also enjoy copy-editing and proofreading other authors' manuscripts.

I've co-authored three humorous fantasy books with Diane Berry: ***Dragons Away!*** (on the strength of which we won the Sir Julius Vogel Award 2012 for Best New Talent), ***Growing Disenchantments*** and ***Fountain of Forever***.

Where I live

Christchurch is a city of approx 400,000 people on the east coast of New Zealand, which is about as far away from anywhere else as it is possible to be.

In September 2010 and February 2011, Christchurch was ravaged by major earthquakes that left much of the central business district in ruins, thousands of people homeless and some parts of the city uninhabitable.

But some of us are still here, writing.

OTHER BOOKS BY THE AUTHOR

Stim

Aspie New Adult contemporary novel (This is the book that precedes Kaleidoscope)

Robert is different. He has Asperger's Syndrome. He experiences the world differently to 99% of the population. Follow his entertaining and highly empathetic story as he struggles to realise and accept who he really is, try to understand other people – which he cannot – and find a girlfriend. Especially find a girlfriend – he's decided it's his special project for the year. Accompanied on this transformative journey by his quirky flatmates, Chloe (who also has Asperger's, amongst other things), Stef (who hasn't, but doesn't mind) and their oddly-named kitten, Robert endures a myriad of awkward moments in his quest to meet a nice, normal girl...and not even a major earthquake will stop him.

This absorbing and humorous story is starkly told from Robert's point of view, through the kaleidoscope of autistic experience.

Co-authored with Diane Berry as K. D. Berry:

Dragons Away!

YA Humorous Fantasy

Only one thing can beat a dragon and that's a bigger dragon. Just his luck that Drewdop is stuck with the job of finding one.

Growing Disenchantments

YA Humorous Fantasy

Releasing the world's most powerful magic talisman aided by an unwilling thief and with a distinct lack of forward planning. What could possibly go wrong?

Fountain of Forever

YA Humorous Fantasy

Time is on the move, mysteriously. Vilnius Baccarat desperately needs some of it. Can the Fountain of Forever save him before his time runs out?

Made in the USA
Charleston, SC
19 November 2015